The Mystery of the
Flaming Footprints

Jupiter Jones was in a fix.

Through no fault of his own, the young detective was locked in a room in a creepy old house. The owner wasn't home. How was Jupe going to get out? He could climb out the window, of course, but he didn't want to look like a burglar. Maybe he could pick the lock.

It sure was hard to be a member of The Three Investigators and stay out of trouble!

Alfred Hitchcock and The Three Investigators in

The Mystery of the Flaming Footprints

Text by M. V. Carey

Based on characters created by Robert Arthur

Illustrated by Harry Kane

 Random House · New York

The Mystery of the Flaming Footprints

Originally published by Random House in 1971
First Random House paperback edition, 1978

Copyright © 1971 by Random House, Inc.
All rights reserved under International and Pan-American Copyright
Conventions. Published in the United States by Random House, Inc.,
New York, and simultaneously in Canada by Random House of
Canada Limited, Toronto.

Library of Congress Cataloging in Publication Data

Carey, M   V
  Alfred Hitchcock and the three investigators in
The mystery of the flaming footprints.

  Summary: When an eccentric local artist disappears suddenly, the
three investigators look into the matter.

  [1. Mystery and detective stories] I. Arthur, Robert. II. Kane,
Harry. III. Title. IV. Title: The mystery of the flaming footprints.
[PZ7.C213Aldf 1978]   [Fic]   78-28742
ISBN 0-394-83776-2

Manufactured in the United States of America
1 2 3 4 5 6 7 8 9 0

Contents

A Word from Alfred Hitchcock

Since it is awkward to be introduced to someone you already know, those of you who are acquainted with The Three Investigators may skip this introduction and proceed directly to Chapter One, where the fun begins.

If you have not yet met Jupiter Jones, Pete Crenshaw, and Bob Andrews, however, a smattering of background information on this remarkable trio may be in order.

Any discussion of The Three Investigators begins with Jupiter Jones, the plump and brainy lad who has no hesitation in admitting that he is the leader of the group—First Investigator and, according to some individuals, chief troublemaker. Jupiter is assisted in his endeavors by Pete Crenshaw, an athletic boy with a prudent desire to avoid danger. This desire is frequently thwarted when Jupiter Jones has a case to solve. The third member of the team is Bob Andrews, a quiet, studious type whose part-time job in the library gives The Three

Investigators quick and expert access to information on almost any subject.

All of these lads reside in Rocky Beach, a small town on the shore of the Pacific Ocean, not too far from Hollywood. Bob Andrews and Pete Crenshaw live with their parents, but Jupiter Jones, who was orphaned when he was very young, makes his home with his aunt and uncle. He assists them in the care and management of The Jones Salvage Yard, the most well-organized junk operation on the entire Pacific Coast.

One must admit that Jupiter occasionally neglects his duties at the salvage yard when there are more exciting things to claim his attention—such as the lonely Potter whom you will encounter shortly, and the bewildered visitors who come to Rocky Beach anticipating a pleasant summer, only to find themselves living in a house which is haunted by a barefooted ghost.

Or is it haunted by something even more sinister?

Of one thing you can be certain, Jupiter Jones and his cohorts will find out.

So much for the introductions. On with the adventure!

ALFRED HITCHCOCK

The Mystery of the
Flaming
Footprints

1

The Potter Appears—
and Disappears

Jupiter Jones heard the truck turn off the Coast Highway. There was no mistaking it. It was The Potter.

Jupe had been raking the white gravel driveway of The Jones Salvage Yard. Now he stopped and listened. "He's coming this way," announced Jupiter.

Aunt Mathilda was nearby, watering the geraniums she had planted along the edge of the drive. She turned the nozzle of the hose, cutting off the flow of water, and looked down the short street toward the highway. "Now why on earth?" wondered Aunt Mathilda.

The Potter's ancient truck wheezed up the very slight grade between the Coast Highway and The Jones Salvage Yard. "He'll never make it," said Aunt Mathilda.

Jupiter grinned. The man who was known in Rocky Beach simply as The Potter was a source of some anxiety to his Aunt Mathilda. Every Saturday morning, The Potter drove his battered old truck into town to pick up his supplies and groceries for the week. Often Aunt Mathilda had been present

3

when the truck coughed and sputtered its way into the parking lot outside the Rocky Beach Market. Always Aunt Mathilda predicted that the ancient vehicle would never be able to groan and puff back up the highway. Always Aunt Mathilda was wrong.

This Saturday was no exception. The truck topped the little grade with steam spouting from the radiator. The Potter waved and swung around the corner and into the salvage yard. Jupe jumped to get his stocky self out of the way, and the truck veered past him and stopped with a tired gasp just inside the gate of the yard.

"Jupiter, my boy!" shouted The Potter. "How are you? And Mrs. Jones! My, you're looking radiant this June morning!"

The Potter fairly bounced out of the cab of his truck, his spotless white robe swirling around him.

Aunt Mathilda could never decide whether or not she approved of The Potter. It was true that he was one of the most skilled craftsmen on the West Coast. People came from as far south as San Diego and as far north as Santa Barbara to buy the pots and jars and vases that he fashioned so beautifully. Aunt Mathilda admired fine craftsmanship. Still, she believed firmly that all male human beings should wear trousers once they had graduated from the romper stage.

The Potter's flowing robes disturbed her sense of things as they should be. So did The Potter's long, gleaming white hair and his neatly combed beard, to say nothing of the ceramic medallion that dangled from a leather thong about his neck. The design on the medallion was a scarlet eagle with two heads. In Aunt Mathilda's opinion, one head per eagle was the right number. The two-headed bird was only another of The Potter's strange whims.

Now Aunt Mathilda looked down at the man's feet with open disapproval. As always, The Potter was barefooted. "You'll step on a nail!" warned Aunt Mathilda.

The Potter only laughed. "I never step on nails, Mrs. Jones," he told her. "You know that. But I could do with some help from you folks today. I am expecting—"

The Potter stopped suddenly and stared at the cabin which served as office for the salvage yard. "What," demanded The Potter, "is that?"

"Mr. Potter," said Aunt Mathilda, "do you mean you haven't seen it? It's months old." She lifted a picture frame down from the office wall and offered it to The Potter for his examination. Under the glass was a series of brightly colored photographs with captions. They had obviously been taken from a magazine. There was one of the front of The Jones Salvage Yard. In the picture, Uncle Titus posed proudly before the wooden fence which surrounded his yard. Artists of Rocky Beach had decorated the fence with a painting of a sailing ship struggling through a stormy, green ocean. In the photograph, one could clearly see a curious painted fish which thrust its head above the waves to watch the ship.

Beneath the photograph of the salvage yard was

a picture of Mr. Dingler, who made silver jewelry in a small shop in Rocky Beach, and one of Hans Jorgenson painting a seascape. And there was one of The Potter himself. The photographer had snapped an excellent close-up of the old man as he emerged from the market, his beard gleaming in the sunlight, his two-headed eagle showing clearly against the white of his robe—and a very ordinary, everyday sack of groceries clutched in one arm. The caption beneath The Potter's photograph pointed out that the residents of Rocky Beach were not disturbed if some of the more artistic citizens took to wearing eccentric garb.

"Surely you knew about it," said Aunt Mathilda. "It's from *Westways* magazine. You remember, they did a photo story on the artists in the beach towns?"

The Potter frowned. "I didn't know," he said. "I remember one day there was a young man with a camera. I didn't pay much attention. We get so many tourists and they all seem to have cameras. If only . . ."

"If only what, Mr. Potter?" asked Aunt Mathilda.

"Nothing," said The Potter. "It can't be helped now." He turned away from Aunt Mathilda and her treasured photo spread and put a hand on Jupe's shoulder. "Jupiter," he said, "I'd like to look through your merchandise. I'm expecting company, and I'm afraid my guests may find my house a little . . . well, a little bare."

"Expecting company?" echoed Aunt Mathilda. "My gracious to heavens!"

In spite of his cheerful, outgoing ways, The Potter had never been known to have a close friend. Jupiter knew that his aunt was wondering mightily who might be coming to visit the old man. However, she refrained from questioning him and simply ordered Jupiter to show him around. "Your Uncle Titus won't be back from Los Angeles for more than an hour," she said, and hurried away to turn off the hose at the faucet.

Jupe was only too happy to show The Potter around. Aunt Mathilda might have her doubts about the old man, but Jupe liked him. "Live and let live" seemed to be his motto, and Jupe thought it was no one's business but The Potter's if he enjoyed bare feet and white robes.

"Now first," said The Potter, "I'll need a couple of bedsteads."

"Yes, sir," said Jupe.

The Jones Salvage Yard was an extremely well-organized operation. It would be hard to imagine any other kind with Aunt Mathilda Jones on the scene. Jupe led The Potter to the shed where used furniture was sheltered from any dampness which might creep in from the ocean. There were bureaus, tables, chairs, and bedsteads. Some of them were broken, or marred by years of use and misuse. There were also pieces which had been refinished or painted by Jupe, his Uncle Titus, and Hans and Konrad, the two Bavarian brothers who helped out in the yard.

The Potter looked over the bedsteads stacked against one wall of the shack. He had purchased new mattresses and springs, he told Jupe, but to his mind springs and a mattress had a very temporary look unless a good solid bedstead was holding them up.

Jupe's curiosity began to get the upper hand. "Are you expecting your company to stay for a long time, Mr. Potter?" he asked.

"I am not sure, Jupiter," said The Potter. "We will have to see. Now what do you think about that brass bed with the scrollwork on the top?"

Jupe was doubtful. "It's very old-fashioned," he told The Potter.

"So am I," announced The Potter. "Who knows? My company may like me that way." He picked up the headboard of the bed and gave it a good shake. "Nice and heavy," he remarked. "They don't make them that way these days. How much?"

Jupe was puzzled. The bed was from an old house in the Hollywood hills. Uncle Titus had bought it just the week before. Jupe had no idea what his uncle planned to ask for it.

"Never mind," said The Potter. "I don't have to know this minute. Put it aside and I'll speak to your uncle when he gets back."

The Potter looked around. "I'll need a second bedstead," he told Jupe. "One for a boy about your age. What would you choose, Jupiter, if you were buying a new bed?"

Jupe didn't hesitate. He hauled out a white wooden bedstead with a bookcase built into it. "If the boy likes to read in bed, this would be perfect," he told The Potter. "The wood is not the best, but Hans sanded it down and painted it. I imagine it looks better now than when it was new."

The Potter was delighted. "Fine! Just fine! And if the boy doesn't read in bed, he can keep his collection on the bookshelf."

"Collection?" questioned Jupe.

"He *must* have a collection," The Potter countered. "Don't all boys collect things? Seashells or stamps or rocks or bottle caps or something?"

Jupe was about to announce that he did not. Then he thought of Headquarters, the old mobile home trailer concealed behind a cunningly arranged pile of junk at the back of the yard. In truth, Jupiter Jones did have a collection. He had a collection of cases solved by The Three Investigators. The records were all in the trailer, neatly preserved in file folders.

"Yes, Mr. Potter, I guess all boys have collections," he said. "Will there be anything else this morning?"

With the question of bedsteads settled, The Potter could not decide what came next. "I have so little in my house," he confessed. "I suppose two more chairs would be in order."

"How many chairs do you have now, Mr. Potter?" asked Jupe gently.

"One," said The Potter. "I have never needed more than one before, and I try not to clutter up my life with things I don't need."

Jupe silently selected two straight chairs from the

pile on the right side of the shack and put them down in front of The Potter.

"A table?" asked Jupiter Jones.

The Potter shook his head. "I have a table. Now, Jupiter, there is that thing called television. I understand that it's extremely popular. My guests might like to have a television, and perhaps you could—"

"No, Mr. Potter," interrupted Jupe. "By the time a set reaches us, we can usually salvage only a few spare parts. If you wish to have a television set, why not buy a new one?"

The Potter looked doubtful.

"New sets are guaranteed," Jupe pointed out. "If they are defective, you can return them to the dealer and have them repaired."

"I see. Well, no doubt you are right, Jupiter. We can make do at first with the beds and the extra chairs. After that—"

The Potter stopped. Outside, in the salvage yard, an automobile horn was blowing violently and repeatedly.

Jupe stepped to the door of the furniture shack. The Potter followed. Parked in the drive, close to The Potter's battered truck, was a gleaming black Cadillac. The horn blared again, and the driver of the car got out, stared around impatiently, then started for the door of the office.

Jupe hurried forward. "Can I help you?" he called.

The man stopped and waited for Jupe and The Potter to come to him. He had, thought Jupiter, a shuttered expression, like one who is used to keeping his thoughts to himself. He was tall and lean and not very old, though a frosting of silver showed here and there in his dark, curling hair.

"Yes, sir?" said Jupe. "You wanted something?"

"I am looking for Hilltop House," said the man. "I seem to have taken the wrong turn off the highway." The man spoke the very precise English of the well-educated European.

"It's a mile north," Jupe told him. "Go back to the highway and turn right. Drive until you see The Potter's place. The lane to Hilltop House is just beyond that. You can't miss it. There's a wooden gate with a padlock."

The man nodded a curt thanks and got back into the car. Then, for the first time, Jupe was aware that there was a second person in the Cadillac. A rather thickset man had been sitting motionless in the back seat. Now he leaned forward to touch the driver's shoulder and say something in a language which Jupe could not understand. The second man seemed neither young nor old nor anywhere in between. He looked ageless. It took Jupe a moment to realize that this was because he was completely bald. Even his eyebrows were gone—if he had ever had eyebrows. And his skin was tanned to the point where it looked like fine leather.

The ageless one glanced at Jupe, then turned his dark, slightly angled eyes to The Potter, who had been standing quietly beside Jupe. The Potter made an odd little hissing sound. Jupe looked at him. He was standing with his head to one side, as if he

were listening intently. His right hand had come up to grip the medallion which hung around his neck.

The ageless man in the car leaned back in his seat. The driver shifted smoothly to reverse and backed out of the driveway. Across the street from the salvage yard, Aunt Mathilda emerged from the house in time to see the Cadillac sweep by and speed back down to the highway.

The Potter touched Jupiter's arm. "My boy," he said, "would you go and ask your aunt if I may have a glass of water? I feel a little dizzy all of a sudden."

The Potter sat down on a pile of lumber. He did look ill.

"I'll get it right away, Mr. Potter," promised Jupe. He hurried across the street.

"Who were those men?" asked Aunt Mathilda.

"They were looking for Hilltop House," said Jupiter. He went into the kitchen, took out the bottle of water that Aunt Mathilda always kept in the refrigerator, and poured a glass for The Potter.

"How peculiar," said Aunt Mathilda. "No one's lived at Hilltop House for years."

"I know," said Jupe. He hurried out with the water. But by the time he got back to the salvage yard, The Potter had disappeared.

2

The Searcher

The Potter's decrepit truck was still in the driveway when Uncle Titus and Hans returned from Los Angeles. They had a load of rusted garden furniture in the back of the salvage-yard truck. Uncle Titus struggled to maneuver his load past The Potter's vehicle, then exploded from the cab of his truck. "What is that thing doing in the middle of the drive?" Uncle Titus demanded.

"The Potter left it when he disappeared," said Jupe.

"When he what?"

"He disappeared," repeated Jupiter.

Uncle Titus sat down on the running board of the truck. "Jupiter, people do not simply disappear."

"The Potter did," said Jupe. "He stopped to buy some furniture to accommodate his expected guests. When he said he was feeling dizzy, I went across to the house and got him a glass of water. While I was gone, he disappeared."

Uncle Titus pulled at his mustache. "Guests?" he said. "The Potter? Disappeared? Disappeared where?"

"It is not difficult to trace the movements of a

14

barefooted man," Jupe told his uncle. "He went out through the gate and down the street. Aunt Mathilda had been watering, and he got his feet wet. At the corner, he turned up toward Coldwell Hill. There are several clear footprints in the dust on the trail that leads up the hill. Unfortunately, he left the trail about fifty yards up and struck off to the north. I found no sign of him after that. The terrain is too rocky to show footprints."

Uncle Titus heaved himself up off the running board. "Well!" he said. He tugged at his mustache and eyed The Potter's truck. "Let's move this wreck out of the drive. We won't do any business with it blocking the way. Let us also pray that The Potter returns soon to claim it."

Uncle Titus made four vain attempts to start The Potter's truck, but the temperamental old engine refused to turn over for him.

"Don't tell *me* machines can't think," declared Uncle Titus. "I wager that The Potter is the only one in creation who can coax any life into this thing."

He climbed down from the truck and motioned Jupe into the driver's seat. Then, with Jupe steering, he and Hans pushed until the truck was safely parked in an empty space next to the office.

Aunt Mathilda had hurried across the road from the house to watch. "I'm going to put The Potter's groceries in our freezer," she decided. "If his things stand out in the sun, they'll spoil. I can't imagine what possesses that man. Jupiter, did he say when his guests were coming?"

"No, he didn't."

Aunt Mathilda took a sack of groceries from the back of the truck. "Jupiter, I think you should take your bike and ride up to The Potter's," she said. "Perhaps The Potter will be there. Or perhaps his company has come. If they're there, Jupiter, bring them back with you. It would be awful to come for a visit and find an empty house."

Jupiter had been about to suggest a trip to The Potter's himself. He grinned and hurried to get his bike.

"And don't dillydally!" Aunt Mathilda called after him. "There's work to be done!"

At that, Jupiter laughed out loud. He pedaled up the highway, keeping well to the right to avoid the cars speeding north, and concluded that The Potter's young guest, if he had arrived, would doubtless be a junior helper in The Jones Salvage Yard before the day was over. Aunt Mathilda knew exactly what to do with boys who were Jupiter's age. Aunt Mathilda put them to work.

The road curved at Evanston Point, and The Potter's house, stark white against the green-black of the California hills, leaped to meet the eye. Jupiter stopped pedaling and coasted. The Potter's place had been an elegant residence once. Now it struck Jupe simply as a brave house, flaunting its Victorian gingerbread on that lonely stretch of coastline.

Jupiter stopped at The Potter's gate. A small sign on the fence proclaimed that The Potter's shop was closed, but that The Potter would return shortly.

Jupiter wondered whether he was even now inside the big white house, unwilling to cope with the usual run of Saturday morning customers. He had certainly looked ill when Jupiter had gone to get the water.

Jupiter leaned his bike against the fence and went in through the gate. The Potter's front yard was paved with flagstones and crowded with tables on which were displayed huge ceramic pieces— large urns, big plaques decorated with flowers or fruit, gigantic vases on which birds hovered in constant, motionless flight.

"Mr. Potter?" called Jupe.

There was no answer. The tall, narrow windows of the old house looked blank. The shed where The Potter kept his supplies was locked and silent. Across the road, parked on the shoulder above the beach, was a dusty tan Ford. There was no one in the car. The owner, no doubt, was on the beach below either surfing or fishing.

The lane which led from the highway up the mountain to Hilltop House was only a few feet beyond The Potter's yard. Jupiter saw that the gate was open. Hilltop House itself was not visible from The Potter's, but Jupe could see the stone wall which supported its terrace. Someone was standing, leaning over that wall. At this distance, Jupe could not tell whether it was the driver of the Cadillac— the man with the dark, curly hair—or his strangely ageless passenger.

Jupe walked quickly past the displays on the wooden tables and up two little steps which were guarded by a pair of urns. The urns were almost as tall as Jupiter himself. A band of double-headed eagles, similar to the eagle on The Potter's medallion, encircled each urn. The eyes glared white in the birds' heads, and the beaks were open as if they screamed defiance at one another.

The wooden porch creaked slightly under Jupe's feet. "Mr. Potter?" he called. "Are you here?"

There was no answer. Jupe frowned. The front door stood slightly open. The Potter, Jupe knew, did not worry greatly about the things in the front yard. They were large and couldn't be easily carried off. But Jupe also knew that everything else The Potter owned was kept securely under lock and key. If the front door was open, The Potter had to be home.

But when Jupe stepped in through the door, the hallway was empty—or as empty as a hallway can be when it is lined, floor to high ceiling, with shelves, and when the shelves are crowded with platters, cups, plates, sugarbowls and cream pitchers, little vases, and colorful candy dishes. The things gleamed, dustless and in perfect order, each one placed so that it would look its very best.

"Mr. Potter?" Jupe was shouting now.

There was no sound, except for the refrigerator which Jupe could hear clicking and humming away in the kitchen. Jupiter looked at the stairs, wondering whether or not he should venture up to the second floor. The Potter might have returned and crept up to bed. He might have fainted.

Then Jupe heard a tiny sound. Something in the

house had stirred. To Jupe's left, as he stood in the hallway, was a closed door. It was, Jupe knew, The Potter's office. The sound had come from there.

"Mr. Potter?" Jupiter rapped at the door.

No one answered. Jupiter put his hand on the doorknob. It turned easily, and the door swung open before Jupe. Except for the roll-top desk in the corner, and the shelves piled high with ledgers and invoice forms, the office was empty. Jupiter went slowly into the room. The Potter did quite a brisk mail-order business. Jupiter saw stacks of price lists and a pile of order forms. A box of envelopes perched on the edge of one shelf.

Then Jupiter saw something which made him catch his breath. The Potter's desk had been forced open. There were fresh scratches on the wood and on the lock which usually secured the roll top. One drawer was open and empty, and file folders were spilled across the desk top.

Someone had been searching The Potter's office.

Jupe started to turn toward the door. Suddenly he felt hands on his shoulders. A foot was thrust between his ankles, and he was shoved, floundering, toward the corner of the room. His head struck the edge of a shelf and he fell, a cascade of papers fluttering down on top of him.

Jupiter was barely aware that a door slammed and a key turned in a lock. Footsteps pounded away across the porch.

Jupe managed to sit up. He waited a moment, afraid that he might be sick. When he was sure that his breakfast would remain where he had put it and that his wits were fairly steady, he got up and stumbled to the window. The Potter's front yard was unoccupied. The searcher, whoever he was, had gotten away.

3

The Potter's Family

There should be a law, thought Jupiter, about telephones. Even eccentric potters should be required to have one.

On the other hand, even if The Potter had had a telephone, it would have been of little use by this time. Whoever had ransacked the office was probably a mile away down the highway now.

Jupiter yanked at the doorknob. The door didn't budge. Jupe went down on one knee and looked through the old-fashioned keyhole. The door had been locked from the outside, and the key was still in the lock. Jupe went to The Potter's desk, found a letter opener, and set to work on the lock.

He could, of course, have gone out through the window, but he preferred not to do that. Jupiter Jones had a well-developed sense of his own dignity. Besides, he knew it would look highly suspicious if anyone on the road outside saw him climbing through a window.

Jupe was prodding at the lock when he heard more footsteps on the porch outside. He froze.

"Grandfather!" shouted someone.

The doorbell rasped rustily in the kitchen.

"Grandfather! It's us!"

Someone knocked on the door.

Jupiter abandoned his efforts with the lock and went to the window. He unlocked it, threw it open, and leaned out. A fair-haired boy stood on the porch, eagerly hammering at the door. Behind him was a youngish woman, her short blonde hair looking untidy and windblown. She held sunglasses in one hand and had an overstuffed brown leather bag slung over her arm.

"Good morning!" said Jupiter Jones.

The woman and the boy stared at him and did not answer.

Jupiter, who had not planned to climb out the window, now very sensibly did just that. He had nothing to lose.

"I was locked in," he explained shortly. He went back into the house through the front door, turned the key in the office door, and threw the door open.

After a slight hesitation, the woman and the boy trailed into the house after Jupiter.

"Someone was searching the office, and I was locked in," he said.

Jupiter surveyed the boy. He was just about Jupe's age. "You must be The Potter's guests," Jupiter announced.

"I am . . . uh . . . say, who are you, anyway?" demanded the boy. "And where's my grandfather?"

"Grandfather?" echoed Jupiter. He looked around for a chair. There was none, so he sat on the stairs.

"Mr. Alexander Potter!" snapped the boy. "This

is his house, isn't it? I asked at the gas station in Rocky Beach, and they said . . ."

Jupe put his elbows on his knees and rested his chin in his hands. His head hurt. "Grandfather?" he said again. "You mean, The Potter has a grandson?"

Jupiter couldn't have been more surprised if someone had told him that The Potter kept a trained dinosaur in his basement.

The woman put on her sunglasses, decided that it was too dark in the hallway, and took the glasses off again. She had a nice face, Jupiter decided. "I don't know where The Potter is," Jupe confessed. "I saw him this morning, but he isn't here now."

"Is that why you were climbing through the window?" demanded the woman. "Tom," she said to the boy, "call the police!"

The boy named Tom looked around, bewildered.

"There's a public telephone on the highway," said Jupiter politely, "just outside the yard."

"You mean my father doesn't have a phone?" demanded the woman.

"If your father is The Potter," said Jupe, "he does not have a telephone."

"Tom!" The woman fumbled in her purse.

"You go call, Mom," said Tom. "I'll stay here and watch this guy!"

"I have no intention of leaving," Jupiter assured them.

The woman went, slowly at first, then running down the path toward the highway.

"So The Potter is your grandfather!" said Jupe.

The boy named Tom glared at him. "What's so weird about it?" he demanded. "Everybody's got a grandfather."

"True," admitted Jupiter. "However, everyone does not have a grandson, and The Potter is . . . well, he's an unusual person."

"I know. He's an artist." Tom stared around at the shelves of ceramics. "He sends us stuff all the time," he told Jupiter.

Jupiter digested this in silence. How long, he wondered, had The Potter been in Rocky Beach? Twenty years, at least, according to Aunt Mathilda. Certainly he had been well-established long before Aunt Mathilda and Uncle Titus had opened The Jones Salvage Yard. The distracted young woman could be his daughter. But, in that case, where had she been all this time? And why had The Potter never spoken of her?

The young woman returned, stuffing a change purse back into her handbag. "There'll be a patrol car right here," she announced.

"Good," said Jupiter Jones.

"And you'll have some explaining to do!" she told Jupiter.

"I'll be glad to explain, Mrs. . . . Mrs. . . ."

"Dobson," said the woman.

Jupiter got to his feet. "I am Jupiter Jones, Mrs. Dobson," he said.

"How do you do," she said, in spite of herself.

"Not too well at the moment," confessed Jupiter. "You see, I came here looking for The Potter, and someone knocked me down and locked me in his office."

Mrs. Dobson's expression indicated that she did not think this a likely story. The wail of a police siren sounded on the highway.

"Rocky Beach doesn't have too many emergencies," said Jupiter calmly. "I am sure Chief Reynolds' men are happy to have a chance to use their siren."

"You're too much!" snorted Tom Dobson.

The siren faltered and died outside the house. Through the open front door, Jupiter saw a black-and-white patrol car come to a stop. Two officers leaped out and hurried up the walk.

Jupiter sat down again on the stairs, and young Mrs. Dobson—her first name was Eloise—introduced herself to the policemen in an absolute avalanche of words. She had, she said, driven all the way from Belleview, Illinois, to visit her father, Mr. Alexander Potter. Mr. Potter was not at home at the moment, and she had found this . . . this juvenile delinquent climbing out of a window. She pointed an accusing finger at Jupe, and suggested that the police might wish to search him.

Officer Haines had lived in Rocky Beach all his life, and Sergeant McDermott had just celebrated his fifteenth year on the force. Both men knew Jupiter Jones. Both men were also well-acquainted with The Potter. Sergeant McDermott made several brief notations on a pad he carried, then said to Eloise Dobson, "Are you prepared to prove that you're The Potter's daughter?"

Mrs. Dobson's face went red, then white. "I beg your pardon?" she cried.

"I said, are you prepared—"

"I heard you the first time!"

"Well, ma'am, if you'll just explain—"

"Explain what? I told you, we came and found this . . . this junior-grade second-story man. . . ."

Sergeant McDermott sighed. "Jupiter Jones may be a pain in the neck," he admitted, "but he doesn't steal things." He favored Jupe with a resigned stare. "What happened, Jones?" he asked. "What were you doing here?"

"Shall I begin at the beginning?" asked Jupiter.

"We've got all day," said McDermott.

So Jupiter began at the beginning. He told of the appearance of The Potter at the salvage yard, and of the purchase of furniture for the expected guests.

Sergeant McDermott nodded at that, and Officer Haines went into the kitchen and brought out the chair, so that Mrs. Dobson could sit down.

Jupe then reported that The Potter had simply walked away from the salvage yard, leaving his truck behind, and had taken to the hills behind Rocky Beach. "I came up to see if he had returned home," said Jupe. "The front door was open and I came in. I did not find The Potter, but someone was hiding in the office. He must have been standing behind the door. When I went in and saw that The Potter's desk had been forced open, whoever it was tripped me from behind and shoved me down. He then ran out and locked the door behind him. Thus it became necessary for me to climb out

through the window when Mrs. Dobson and her
son appeared and rang the bell."

Sergeant McDermott waited a moment, then
said, "Huh!"

"The Potter's office has been searched," Jupe insisted. "You will see that his papers are upset."

McDermott stepped to the office door and
looked in at the files spread on the desk, and at the
desk drawer sagging open.

"The Potter is extremely orderly," Jupe pointed
out. "He would never leave his office in that condition."

McDermott turned back to the group in the hallway. "We'll get the fingerprint man up here," he
announced. "In the meantime, Mrs. Dobson—"

At which, Eloise Dobson burst into tears.

"Hey, Mom!" The boy named Tom moved close
and put a hand on her arm. "Hey, Mom, don't!"

"Well, he *is* my father!" sobbed Mrs. Dobson. "I
don't care! He is, and we drove all the way to see
him and we didn't even stop at the Grand Canyon
because I wanted . . . because I can't even remember . . ."

"Mom!" pleaded Tom Dobson.

Mrs. Dobson dug into her purse for a tissue.
"Well, I didn't expect I'd have to prove it!" she
cried. "I didn't know you needed a birth certificate
to get into Rocky Beach!"

"Now, Mrs. Dobson!" Sergeant McDermott
folded his notebook and put it into his pocket.
"Under the circumstances, it might be best if you
and your son did not remain here."

"But Alexander Potter *is* my father!"

"That may be," conceded the sergeant, "but it looks as if he's decided to make himself scarce—at least for the moment. And it appears that someone has entered the house illegally. I'm sure that The . . . that Mr. Potter will show up, sooner or later, and explain things. But in the meantime, you and the boy would be safer if you stayed in the village. There's the Seabreeze Inn, and it's very nice and—"

"Aunt Mathilda would be glad to have you," put in Jupiter.

Mrs. Dobson ignored him. She sniffled and dabbed at her eyes, her hands shaking.

"Besides," said McDermott, "the fingerprint man will be here, and we don't want anything disturbed."

"Where is this Seabreeze Inn?" asked Mrs. Dobson.

"Down the road a mile and a half to the village," said McDermott. "You'll see the sign."

Mrs. Dobson got up and put her sunglasses on.

"Chief Reynolds may want to talk to you later," said McDermott. "I'll tell him he can find you at the inn."

Mrs. Dobson began to cry again. Young Tom hurried her out of the house and down the path to the road, where she got behind the wheel of a blue convertible with Illinois license plates.

"Now I've seen everything!" said Sergeant McDermott. "The Potter's daughter!"

"If she *is* The Potter's daughter," said Officer Haines.

"Why would she fake it?" said McDermott. "The Potter's a real kook, and he's got nothing anybody wants."

"He must have something," said Jupiter Jones, "or why would someone go to the trouble to search his office?"

4

Too Many Newcomers

Jupiter refused Haines's offer of a ride back to Rocky Beach. "I've got my bike," he told the policeman. "And I'm okay."

Haines squinted at the bruise on Jupe's forehead. "You sure?" he asked.

"I'm sure. It's just a bump." Jupiter started down the path.

"Well, watch it, Jones!" McDermott called after him from the house. "You keep poking your nose in where it doesn't belong, you'll get it cut off one of these days. And stick close to home, you hear? The chief will probably want to talk to you, too."

Jupiter waved, picked up his bicycle, and stood waiting for a break in the traffic so that he could cross the highway. The tan Ford which Jupe had noticed earlier was still parked on the shoulder above the beach. The traffic slackened, and Jupe raced across the road with his bicycle. He stood beside the car and looked down at the beach. The tide was going out, leaving broad stretches of wet sand. Coming up the path toward him was the most magnificent fisherman Jupe had ever seen. He had on a sparkling white turtleneck shirt and, over it, a spotless pale blue jacket with a crest on the pocket. The jacket exactly matched his pale blue duck trousers and these, in turn, blended beautifully with his blue sneakers. He wore a yachting cap so immaculate it might have been taken off the shelf at the sporting goods store only yesterday.

"Hello, there!" said the man, as he came abreast of Jupe. Jupe saw a thin, tanned face, oversized sunglasses, and a gray mustache, waxed so that the ends pointed out and up toward the man's ears.

. The man's fishing tackle and creel were as perfect, as gleaming bright as the rest of him.

"Any luck?" asked Jupiter Jones.

"No. They're not biting today." The man opened the trunk of the dusty Ford and began to stow his gear. "Maybe I'm not using the right bait. I'm new at this."

Jupiter had already guessed that. Most fishermen, he knew, looked like refugees from the Good Will store.

The man looked across at the patrol car parked in front of The Potter's house. "Excitement?" he asked.

"A little," said Jupiter. "A housebreaker, probably."

"How dull." The lid of the trunk thumped closed.

The man unlocked the car door on the driver's side. "Isn't that the shop of the very famous Potter?" he said.

Jupe nodded.

"He a friend of yours?" asked the fisherman. "You live around here?"

"Yes, I live around here. I know him. Everybody in town knows The Potter."

"Hm. I should think so. Does beautiful work, I understand." Behind the sunglasses, the eyes went over Jupe from head to toe. "Nasty bump you've got there."

"I fell," said Jupe shortly.

"I see. Can I give you a lift anywhere?"

"No, thank you," said Jupiter.

"No? Well, you're right. Never take rides from a stranger, eh?" The man laughed as if he had just said something terribly funny, then started his car, backed onto the highway, waved at Jupe, and drove off.

Jupe rode back to the salvage yard. He did not, however, go in through the main gates. Instead he continued on down the length of the wonderfully painted fence until he came to the curious fish poking its head up from the sea to watch the ship sailing through the furious storm. Jupiter got off his bike and pressed on the eye of the fish. Two boards swung up, and Jupe pushed his bicycle ahead of him into the salvage yard.

This was Green Gate Number One. In all, there were four secret entrances to The Jones Salvage Yard—and Aunt Mathilda Jones was unaware of the existence of any of them. Jupiter, emerging in the corner of the junkyard by his outdoor workshop, could hear Aunt Mathilda. She was evidently out behind the furniture shed, applying herself to cleaning up the recently purchased garden furniture. And she was urging Hans, with some vigor, to

do likewise. She could not see Jupiter because he had cleverly arranged the piles of junk in front of his workshop to block the view. Jupe grinned, propped his bike against an old printing press, pulled aside a cast-iron grate which leaned against a workbench behind the printing press, and bent to crawl into Tunnel Two.

Tunnel Two was a length of corrugated iron pipe. It was padded inside with odd scraps of carpeting, and it led to a trapdoor in the trailer which was Headquarters for The Three Investigators. Jupe crawled the length of Tunnel Two, climbed up through the trapdoor, and reached for the telephone on the desk in the trailer.

The telephone was another improvement in The Jones Salvage Yard of which Aunt Mathilda was unaware. Jupiter and his friends, Bob Andrews and Pete Crenshaw, paid for it with money they earned working in the salvage yard, and with occasional fees The Three Investigators collected for solving a case.

Now Jupiter dialed Pete's number. Pete answered after only two rings. "Hey, Jupe!" Pete seemed delighted to hear from Jupiter. "Surf 'll be up this afternoon. What do you say we take our boards and—"

"I doubt that I will have an opportunity to do any surfing today," said Jupiter dourly.

"Oh? You mean your aunt's on the warpath?"

"Uncle Titus acquired several pieces of garden furniture today," said Jupiter. "They are badly rusted, and Aunt Mathilda is now directing Hans on the removal of rust and old paint. I am certain that when she sees me, I shall join Hans."

Pete, who was accustomed to Jupiter's precise method of speech, simply wished him happy paint-removal.

"That is not why I called," Jupiter informed him. "Can you come to Headquarters tonight at nine?"

Pete could and would.

"Red Gate Rover," said Jupiter simply, and hung up.

He then dialed Bob Andrews' home. Mrs. Andrews answered. Bob was at his part-time job at the Rocky Beach Public Library.

"May I leave a message, Mrs. Andrews?" asked Jupe.

"Of course, Jupiter, but I'd better get a pencil and write it down. You boys never seem to say anything in plain English."

Jupiter did not comment on this. He waited while Mrs. Andrews hunted up a pencil and a piece of paper, and then said, "Red Gate Rover at nine."

"Red Gate Rover at nine," repeated Mrs. Andrews. "Whatever that may mean. All right, Jupiter, I'll tell him when he gets home."

Jupiter thanked her, hung up, and retreated out of Headquarters and back down Tunnel Two. He opened Green Gate One, pushed his bike onto the street, and rode up to the gravel drive of The Jones Salvage Yard.

Aunt Mathilda was waiting beside the office,

stained rubber gloves on her hands. "I was about to send the police after you," she announced. "What happened?"

"The Potter wasn't there," Jupe told her. "His company came, though."

"They did? Why didn't you bring them back with you? Jupiter, I told you to invite them!"

Jupiter parked his bicycle next to the office. "They are not sure whether or not I am Jack the Ripper," he told his aunt. "They have gone to the Seabreeze Inn. One of them is a lady named Dobson who says she is The Potter's daughter, and the other is her son Tom."

"The Potter's daughter? Jupiter, that's ridiculous. The Potter never had a daughter!"

"Are you sure?" asked Jupe.

"Well, of course. He never mentioned . . . he never . . . Jupiter, why should they think you're Jack the Ripper?"

Jupiter explained, as briefly as he could, about the intruder in The Potter's office. "They think I broke into the house," he finished.

"The very idea!" Aunt Mathilda bristled with indignation. "And look at your head. Jupiter, go in the house this minute. I'll get you an ice pack."

"Aunt Mathilda, it's all right, really."

"It is not all right. In the house. Now! Go!"

Jupiter went.

Aunt Mathilda brought him an ice pack. Also a peanut-butter sandwich and a glass of milk. By dinner time she had decided that his bump on the head was no worse than any one of a hundred other bumps he had survived. She clattered through the dinner dishes, left Jupiter to dry and put away, and went to wash her hair.

Uncle Titus gratefully went to sleep in front of the television set, and when Jupiter tiptoed out of the house, his big mustache was vibrating softly to the rhythm of his snores.

Jupiter crossed the street and circled around to the back of the salvage yard. The yard's back fence was as fancifully decorated as the front fence. The painting depicted the great San Francisco fire of 1906, with terrified people fleeing from burning buildings. In the foreground of the scene, a little dog sat watching the excitement. One of his eyes was a knot in the wooden board. Jupiter deftly picked the knot out of the board, reached through the hole to undo a catch, and three boards swung open. This was Red Gate Rover. Inside, a sign with a black arrow pointed the way to "Office." Jupiter followed the direction of the arrow, crept under a pile of lumber, and came out into a corridor with junk piled high on every side. He made his way along the corridor until he came to several heavy planks which formed the roof of Door Four. He had only to get under these, crawl a few feet, and push on a panel—and he was in Headquarters.

Eight forty-five. He waited, reviewing the events of the day in his mind. At ten of nine Bob Andrews wriggled into the trailer. Pete Crenshaw put in his appearance promptly at nine.

"Do The Three Investigators have another client?" asked Pete brightly. He looked at the bruise on Jupe's forehead. "Like you, maybe?"

"Possibly," said Jupiter Jones. "Today The Potter disappeared."

"I heard about that," said Bob. "Your Aunt Mathilda sent Hans down to the market to pick up some stuff. He met my mother. Just walked away and left his truck here?"

Jupiter nodded. "That is exactly what he did. The truck is still parked beside the office. The Potter disappeared, and a number of other people appeared."

"Such as that woman who checked into the Seabreeze Inn after you got bonked on the bean?" questioned Pete.

"Rocky Beach is indeed a small town," murmured Jupiter.

"I met Officer Haines," Pete explained. "She claims she's The Potter's daughter. If she is, that kid with her must be his grandson. Crazy! That Potter's a funny old guy. You'd sure never suspect he had a daughter."

"He must have been young once," said Jupiter. "But Mrs. Dobson and her son are not the only newcomers in Rocky Beach. There are two men at Hilltop House."

"Hilltop House?" Pete straightened up. "Has somebody moved into Hilltop House? That place is a wreck!"

"Someone at least visited there today," said Jupiter. "It was an interesting coincidence that they stopped at the salvage yard this morning to ask directions. The Potter was there at the time, which may also be an interesting coincidence. They saw him, and he saw them. And Hilltop House directly overlooks The Potter's shop."

"Did he know them?" asked Bob.

Jupe pulled at his lip, trying to recall every detail of the scene. "I could not say with any certainty that he did, or that they knew him. The driver, who seemed to be European, asked for directions, and the passenger—an odd-looking person with a completely bald head—became somewhat excited. They talked together for a moment in a foreign language. The Potter stood there, holding onto that medallion he always wears. After they left, he said he felt ill. I went to get him some water, and he disappeared."

"He was okay when he came into the yard?" asked Bob.

"Very okay," confirmed Jupiter. "He was expecting company, and he seemed pleased. But after the men came and asked about Hilltop House—"

"He disappeared!" said Bob.

"Yes. He walked away. Now I wonder, was he only holding that medallion out of habit, the way one would twist a button perhaps, or was he trying to cover it up?"

"It's an eagle, isn't it?" asked Bob.

"An eagle with two heads," said Jupiter. "It could be a design The Potter made up, or it could be something more—a symbol that meant something to the men in the car."

"Like a signal?" asked Pete.

"Or a crest," decided Bob. "Europeans are big on crests, and they have all kinds of things on them, like lions and unicorns and falcons and such."

"Can you check it out?" Jupiter asked. "Do you remember what it looked like?"

Bob nodded. "There's a new book on heraldry in at the library. If I see that double-headed eagle again, I'll recognize it."

"Good." Jupiter turned to Pete. "You're friendly with Mr. Holtzer?" he asked.

"The real estate man? I mow his lawn once in a while, when he doesn't feel like doing it himself. Why?"

"He has the only real estate agency in Rocky Beach," said Jupiter. "If someone has moved into Hilltop House, he will know it. He may also know who and why."

"He probably won't want his lawn mowed tomorrow," said Pete, "but he's open on Sunday. I'll drop in and see him."

"Fine," said Jupiter. "I believe that Aunt Mathilda wishes to go to the Seabreeze Inn tomorrow. She will be a one-woman welcoming committee for Mrs. Dobson and her son. I will accompany her, and will also keep an eye out for an amateur fisherman in a tan Ford."

"Another newcomer?" said Bob.

Jupiter shrugged. "Perhaps. Or perhaps he only came down from Los Angeles for the day. If he is staying in Rocky Beach, and if Hilltop House has been rented, we know that we have five new people in town in one day—and one of them may have broken into The Potter's house."

5

The Flaming Footprints

"Wear your white shirt, Jupiter," ordered Aunt Mathilda, "and your blue blazer."

"It's too hot for a blazer," said Jupe.

"Wear it anyway," said Aunt Mathilda. "I'd prefer not to have you look like a second-story man when we call on Mrs. Dobson."

Jupiter sighed and buttoned the starched white shirt almost to the neck. The top button was impossible. He would have choked if he'd tried it. He shrugged himself into his blue blazer.

"Are you ready?" he asked his aunt.

Aunt Mathilda smoothed down a tweed skirt which was so sturdy that it almost prickled and threw a tan cardigan around her shoulders. "How do I look?"

"Not a bit like the aunt of a second-story man," Jupiter assured her.

"I certainly hope not," said Aunt Mathilda, and they went downstairs and out through the living room. Uncle Titus had voted himself out of the welcoming party for the Dobsons. He was taking his Sunday afternoon nap on the sofa.

A fresh breeze had sprung up to blow away the

morning fog, and the sun sparkled on the ocean as Aunt Mathilda and Jupiter walked down to the highway and then turned south. There were few people on the sidewalks in the business district of Rocky Beach, but there was a solid procession of cars edging through the town. Jupiter and his aunt passed the Rocky Beach Bakery and the delicatessen, and came to the crosswalk opposite the Seabreeze Inn.

"Miss Hopper does keep the inn very nicely," said Aunt Mathilda. She stepped into the crosswalk and directed a no-nonsense glare at the radiator of an oncoming Buick. The driver of the Buick, properly cowed, applied his brakes, and Aunt Mathilda plowed on across the highway with Jupiter hurrying in her wake.

Aunt Mathilda strode into the office of the Seabreeze Inn and rapped at the little bell on Miss Hopper's registration desk.

A door behind the desk opened. "Mrs. Jones!" cried Miss Hopper. She emerged, tucking in a stray wisp of white hair. She carried with her a distinct odor of roasting chicken. "Jupiter, nice to see you."

"I understand that Mrs. Dobson and her son are staying with you," said Aunt Mathilda, getting right to the point.

"Oh yes, poor dear thing. What a state she was in when she checked in yesterday. And then Chief Reynolds came to see her, right here in the inn! Imagine!"

Miss Hopper appreciated Chief Reynolds' service to the citizens of Rocky Beach, but it was plain that she did not care to have the police invade her little inn.

Aunt Mathilda made a clucking sound to indicate that she understood Miss Hopper's position. She asked again for Mrs. Dobson, and was directed to the little terrace behind the inn. "She and the boy are there, and that nice Mr. Farrier is trying to cheer them up," said Miss Hopper.

"Mr. Farrier?" echoed Jupiter.

"One of my guests," explained Miss Hopper. "Charming person. Seems to take a real interest in Mrs. Dobson. It's nice, don't you think? Nowadays, people don't seem to care about one another. Of course, Mrs. Dobson's a very pretty young woman."

"That always helps," said Aunt Mathilda.

She and Jupiter went out of the office and walked back along the verandah of the inn, past numbered doors and blue-shuttered windows, to the little terrace that looked out over the beach to the ocean.

Young Mrs. Dobson and her son were sitting at a small round table on the terrace, soft drinks in paper cups in front of them. With them was the jaunty, mustached fisherman whom Jupiter had met on the highway the day before. If possible, he was more magnificent than he had been when Jupe first saw him. His jacket and his duck trousers were a sparkling, crackling white. His yachting cap was pushed back on his head, so that a lock of iron-gray hair showed. He was telling Mrs. Dobson of the wonders of Hollywood, and offering to be her guide should she wish to take a little tour. From the glazed look in Mrs. Dobson's eyes, he had been at it for some time.

He had not, decided Jupiter, cheered Mrs. Dobson up. He was only boring her to death. Eloise Dobson looked profoundly grateful at the sight of Jupe escorting his aunt onto the terrace.

"Hi!" shouted young Tom Dobson, who leaped up to get another couple of chairs.

"Mrs. Dobson," Jupiter began, "my aunt and I—"

Aunt Mathilda firmly took the introductions into her own hands. "I am Mrs. Titus Jones," she informed Mrs. Dobson. "Jupiter's aunt. I have come to assure you that Jupiter would never, under any circumstances, break into Mr. Potter's residence."

Tom Dobson placed a chair at the table and Aunt Mathilda sat down.

Eloise Dobson smiled a tired smile. "I'm sure he wouldn't," she said. "Sorry I flew out at you like a rusty shutter yesterday, Jupiter. I was just tired, I guess, and nervous. We'd driven straight through from Arizona, and I hadn't seen my father since I was a baby." She turned the paper cup on the table. "I guess you could say I've never seen him. You don't remember much that happened when you were three. I wasn't sure what to expect, and then when we arrived and found you climbing out the window, I thought—well, I thought you'd broken in."

"Naturally," said Jupiter. He sat down, and

young Tom hurried off to the soft drink machine with a handful of dimes.

"And then the police behaved so strangely, and no one seemed to believe I am who I am," continued Mrs. Dobson. "And Father disappearing the way he did. I didn't sleep a lot last night, I can tell you."

Mr. Farrier murmured, "I should think not, my dear." He made a move as if to take Mrs. Dobson's hand. She quickly put it under the table. "This is Mr. Farrier," she said, not quite looking at him. "Mr. Farrier, Mrs. Jones—and Jupiter Jones."

"Jupiter Jones and I have met," said Farrier heartily. "How's the head, young friend?"

"Very well, thank you," answered Jupiter.

"Have to be careful about falls," said Farrier. "I remember the time I was in Cairo—"

"Never been there!" snapped Aunt Mathilda, who did not want this intruder running off with the conversation.

Mr. Farrier closed his mouth.

"Mrs. Dobson, what do you plan to do now?" Aunt Mathilda asked.

Mrs. Dobson sighed. "I'm certainly not going to go back to Belleview without finding out what happened," she said bravely. "Luckily, I have a letter from my father telling me that I am welcome here for the summer—if I insist on coming. It isn't the warmest invitation I ever had, but it *is* an invitation. I showed it to Chief Reynolds this morning. It's on Father's letterhead, so he knows I'm telling the truth. He has a man on guard at the house, but

he says the fingerprint men are through there, and
if we want to move in, he won't try to stop us. But
I don't think he likes the idea."

"Are you going to do it?" asked Aunt Mathilda.

"I think so. The trip's been expensive, and we
can't stay here at the inn for nothing, and Tom's
going to start clucking if he eats one more piece of
fried chicken at a roadside restaurant. Mrs. Jones,
why can't the chief send a search party into the
hills to find my father?"

Jupiter stirred. "It wouldn't be practical, Mrs.
Dobson," he said. "Obviously The Potter disappeared because he wanted to disappear, and there
are a thousand places in those hills where he could
hide out. Even in his bare feet, he could—"

"Bare feet?" said Eloise Dobson.

There was a short, unhappy silence. Then Aunt
Mathilda said, "You didn't know?"

"Know what? Did he leave his shoes behind, or
what?"

"The Potter never wears shoes," said Aunt Mathilda.

"You're joking!"

"I am sorry," said Aunt Mathilda, and she was.
"He does not wear shoes. He goes about in his bare
feet and a white robe." Aunt Mathilda stopped, not
wishing to add to Mrs. Dobson's distress. Then she
decided she might as well complete the description.
"He has long white hair and rather a full beard."

Young Tom Dobson had returned with drinks
for Aunt Mathilda and Jupiter. "Sounds like the
prophet Elijah," he decided.

"In other words," said Mrs. Dobson, "my father is the town eccentric."

"He's only one of many," Jupiter assured her. "Rocky Beach has its full share of eccentrics."

"I see." There was a soda straw on the table. Mrs. Dobson picked it up and began folding it into waxy pleats. "No wonder he never sent pictures of himself. He was probably nervous about my coming. I don't think he liked the idea a lot, but I did want to see him. So I suppose, when the time actually came, he got scared and lit out. Well, he's not going to get away with it. I'm his daughter and I'm here and I'm going to stay, and he darn well better show up."

"You tell 'em, Mom!" applauded young Tom.

"So there's no sense in wasting time," said Eloise Dobson. "Tom, you go and tell Miss Hopper we're checking out this afternoon. And call that police chief. He'll have to notify his guard to let us into the house."

"Are you sure you are doing the wise thing?" asked Jupiter. "I didn't break into The Potter's yesterday, but someone did. I have a bump on the head to prove it."

Eloise Dobson stood up. "I intend to be careful," she told Jupe. "And anyone who comes snooping around had better be careful, too. I don't believe in guns, but I'm handy with a baseball bat, and I brought one with me."

Aunt Mathilda regarded her with open admiration. "How clever. I wouldn't have thought of it."

Jupiter wanted to laugh out loud. His Aunt Mathilda wouldn't need a baseball bat. If they had an intruder at The Jones Salvage Yard, Aunt Mathilda would probably swat him with a second-hand bureau.

Aunt Mathilda now surged to her feet. "If you are going to move into The Potter's house today, you'll need your furniture," she said. "He stopped at our salvage yard yesterday and selected a bedstead for you and one for your son—and a couple of other things. Jupiter and I will attend to it. We'll meet you at the house in half an hour. Will that be time enough?"

"Plenty of time," said Mrs. Dobson. "You're very kind. I hate to trouble you."

"Not at all," said Aunt Mathilda. "Come, Jupiter." She started down the verandah toward the street, and then remembered something. She turned back toward the terrace. "Good afternoon, Mr. Farrier," she called.

Jupiter and Aunt Mathilda were halfway back to the salvage yard before Jupe allowed himself to laugh out loud. "I wonder whether that guy Farrier has ever been so completely ignored," he said to his aunt. "You ran over him like a Sherman tank."

"Silly ass!" snapped Aunt Mathilda. "I am sure he was bothering that poor girl. . . . Men!"

Aunt Mathilda stormed into the house to rouse Uncle Titus from his Sunday afternoon stupor. Uncle Titus, in turn, called Hans and Konrad, and in fifteen minutes the salvage-yard truck was loaded with the bedsteads selected by The Potter, the two straight chairs, plus two small bureaus which Aunt Mathilda herself hauled from the furniture shed. "She'll need something to unpack her things into," said Aunt Mathilda.

Hans and Jupiter gathered up The Potter's groceries, and then Aunt Mathilda, Hans, and Jupe squeezed into the cab of the truck and headed up the highway toward The Potter's house.

The blue convertible with the Illinois plates was standing near the shed where The Potter kept his supplies when Aunt Mathilda drove the truck in off the highway. Young Tom Dobson was carrying two suitcases into the house, and Mrs. Dobson stood on the porch, the wind ruffling her short hair.

"Everything all right?" called Aunt Mathilda.

"Well, fingerprint powder is gray, in case you were wondering," said Eloise Dobson. "And it's all over the place. It'll clean up, I suppose. But outside of about six zillion dishes, this place is bare as a barn."

"The Potter did not believe in encumbering himself with possessions," Jupiter explained.

Eloise Dobson shot him a curious glance. "Do you always talk like that?" she asked.

"Jupiter reads a great deal," explained Aunt Mathilda, and she went around to the back of the truck to supervise the unloading of the furniture.

Jupiter, struggling with the heavy brass headboard, saw two men stroll down the lane from Hilltop House. They were the two visitors of the day before—the thin dark-haired man and the heavier, bald person. Both were wearing neat business suits

and black oxfords. They glanced at the activity in
The Potter's yard, then crossed the highway and
disappeared down the path to the beach.

Tom Dobson came around to give Jupe a hand.
"Who are they?" he asked. "Neighbors?"

"I'm not sure," said Jupiter. "They're new in
town."

Tom got hold of one side of the headboard and
Jupiter hefted the other. "Funny outfits for beach-
walking," said Tom.

"Not everybody dresses the part," said Jupiter,
thinking of the magnificently costumed Mr. Farrier.

Tom and Jupiter staggered into the house with
the headboard and up the stairs, and Jupiter saw
that Eloise Dobson had spoken the truth. The Potter's house was barer than most barns. There were
four bedrooms on the second floor, and a bath with
an old-fashioned tub set high on claw legs. In one
bedroom was a narrow cot, neatly made up and
covered with a white spread. The Potter also had a
small bedside table, a lamp, a wind-up alarm clock
and a little three-drawer chest painted white. That
was all. The other three rooms were immaculate,
but completely empty.

"You want this one, Mom?" called Tom, poking
his head into the front room.

"Doesn't matter," said Mrs. Dobson.

"It's got a fireplace," said Tom. "And wow, look
at that wild thing!"

Tom and Jupiter leaned the headboard against

the wall and looked at that wild thing. It was a ceramic plaque, fully five feet across. It was set flush with the wall above the fireplace.

"The double-headed eagle!" said Jupiter Jones.

Tom cocked his head to one side and examined the scarlet bird, screeching from both pointed beaks. "Old friend of yours?" he asked Jupiter.

"Possibly an old friend of your grandfather's," said Jupiter. "He always wore a medallion with that design on it. It must have meant something special to him. There are rows of double-headed eagles on those two big urns by the front steps. Did you notice them?"

"I was busy," said Tom. "We had a bed to move." Aunt Mathilda's footsteps were heavy on the stairs. "I hope that man thought to get enough sheets," worried Aunt Mathilda. "And pads for the beds. Jupiter, did you see mattresses anywhere?"

"They're in the back room," called Tom. "Brand new. Still have the paper around them."

"Thank goodness," declared Aunt Mathilda. She yanked open doors until she found the linen closet, and there were the sheets, also new, and pads for the beds, and blankets. And two new pillows still encased in plastic.

Aunt Mathilda threw open one of the front windows. "Hans!" she called.

"Coming!" Hans was making his way up the front steps, the footboard of the brass bed balanced on his head.

"That will be a stinker to put up," said Tom Dobson.

It was. It took the combined efforts of Tom, Jupiter, and Hans to get the big bed firmly erect on its four legs. Then springs and mattress were carried in from the back room and put in place, and Aunt Mathilda began unfolding sheets.

"Oh, the groceries!" she said suddenly. "They're still in back of the truck."

"Groceries?" said Mrs. Dobson. "Mrs. Jones, you shouldn't have done that."

"I didn't," Aunt Mathilda informed her. "Your father bought enough food to take Sherman's Army clear to the sea. I had it in my freezer so it wouldn't spoil."

Eloise Dobson looked perplexed. "Father certainly seems prepared for us. So why did he run off? . . . Well, I'll get the groceries," she said quickly, and went out of the room and down the stairs.

"Jupiter, give her a hand," ordered Aunt Mathilda.

Jupiter was halfway down the stairs when Mrs. Dobson came in, brown paper sacks in her arms. "We won't go hungry, anyway," she announced, and marched toward the kitchen.

Jupiter was close behind her when she suddenly stopped dead. Her arms went limp, and the sacks thumped to the floor.

Then Eloise Dobson screamed.

Jupiter pushed her to one side and stared past her into the kitchen. Near the pantry door, three weird, eerie green flames leaped and flickered.

"What is it?" Aunt Mathilda and Tom thundered down the stairs. Hans came behind them.

Jupiter and Mrs. Dobson were frozen, staring at those tongues of ghostly green fire.

"Gracious to heavens!" gasped Aunt Mathilda.

The flames sputtered and sank, then died, leaving not a wisp of smoke.

"What the heck?" said Tom Dobson.

Jupiter, Hans, and Tom shoved forward into the kitchen. For almost a minute they looked at the linoleum—at the places where the flames had danced. Then Hans said it. "The Potter! He came back! He came back to haunt the house!"

"Impossible!" said Jupiter Jones.

But he could not deny that there, charred into the linoleum, were three footprints—and they were the prints of naked feet.

6

The Investigators
Have a Client

Hans was immediately sent to the telephone box on the highway to summon the police, who appeared within minutes and searched the house from attic to cellar and found nothing—nothing but the strange, charred footprints in the kitchen.

Officer Haines sniffed at the footprints, measured them, dug a few bits of burned linoleum out of the floor and put them into an envelope. He gave Jupiter a cool look. "If you know anything about this, and you're holding out on us—" he began.

"Ridiculous!" snapped Aunt Mathilda. "How could Jupiter know anything we don't know? He has been with me all day, and he was just going downstairs to help Mrs. Dobson with the groceries when those—those footprints appeared."

"Okay. Okay," said the officer. "Only he has this habit, Mrs. Jones. He's always around when trouble happens."

Haines put the envelope with the burned bits of linoleum in his pocket. "If I were you, Mrs. Dobson," he said, "I'd get out of here and go back to the inn."

Eloise Dobson sat down and began to cry, and

Aunt Mathilda angrily ran water into a kettle and set about making a heartening cup of tea. Aunt Mathilda believed there were few crises in life which could not be eased by a good hot cup of tea.

The police departed for headquarters. Tom and Jupiter went quietly out into the big front yard and sat on the steps between the two huge urns.

"I'm almost ready to think Hans was right," said Tom. "Suppose my grandfather is dead, and . . ."

"I do not believe in ghosts," said Jupiter firmly. "What's more, I don't think you believe in them, either. And The Potter made great preparations for your visit. Why should he return and frighten your mother that way?"

"I'm scared, too," Tom admitted, "and if my grandfather isn't dead, where is he?"

"The last we knew, he was up in the hills," said Jupiter.

"But why?" demanded Tom.

"That may depend on a great many things," Jupiter said. "How much do you really know about your grandfather?"

"Not much," admitted young Tom. "Just what I've heard my mother say. And she doesn't know much herself. One thing, his name wasn't always Potter."

"Oh?" said Jupiter. "I have always wondered about that. It seemed too coincidental."

"He came to the United States a long time ago," Tom said. "About 1931 or so. He was a Ukrainian and he had a name that was so full of c's and z's that nobody could pronounce it. He was taking ceramics at a night school in New York when he met my grandmother, and she didn't want to be Mrs. . . . Mrs. . . . well, whatever it was, so he changed his name to Potter."

"Your grandmother was a New Yorker?" asked Jupiter.

"Not really," said Tom. "She was born in Belleview, just like us. She went to New York to design clothes or something. Then she met this Alexander Whosis and she married him. I don't suppose he wore a long white robe in those days. She wouldn't have gone for that. She was pretty square."

"You remember her?"

"A little. She died a long time ago. I was only a kid. Pneumonia. From what I've heard, in the family you know, she and my grandfather didn't hit it off from the beginning. He was real good at ceramics, and he had a little shop, but she said he was awfully nervous, and had three locks on every door. And she said she could not stand the forevermore smell of wet clay. So when my mother was going to be born, she came back to Belleview, and she stayed."

"She never returned to her husband?"

"Nope. I think he came to see her once, when my mother was a baby, but she never went back to him."

Jupiter pulled at his lip and thought of The Potter, so alone in his house by the sea.

"He never gave up on her," said young Tom. "He sent money every month—for my mother, you know. And when my folks were married, he sent them a terrific tea set. And he never stopped writing. Even after my grandmother died, he wrote to my mother. Still does."

"And your father?" asked Jupiter.

"Oh, he's a great guy," said Tom happily. "He runs the hardware store in Belleview. He didn't exactly go into fits of joy when Mom decided to come out here and see Grandfather, but she argued him around to it."

"I don't suppose you know why your grandfather came to California," said Jupiter.

"The weather, I suppose," said Tom. "Isn't that why most people come?"

"There are other reasons," Jupiter told him. His eyes were on the path to the beach. The two dark-clad men came floundering up the path, crossed the highway, and started to walk up the lane to Hilltop House.

Jupiter stood up and leaned against one of the urns, tracing the pattern of the screaming scarlet eagles with a forefinger. "An interesting series of puzzles," he remarked. "First, why did The Potter choose to disappear? Second, who searched his office yesterday? Also, who, or what, caused those flaming footprints in the kitchen? And why? And isn't it curious that no one in Rocky Beach even knew you existed?"

"But if he was a hermit?" said young Tom. "I mean, a guy who only has one chair in his house isn't exactly running a social club."

"Hermit or no hermit," said Jupiter Jones, "he was also a grandfather. A number of Aunt Mathilda's friends are grandparents, and they're always showing off snapshots of their grandchildren. The Potter never, never did that. He never even mentioned you or your mother to anyone."

Tom hunched forward and hugged his knees. "Makes you feel invisible," he declared. "This thing's like some kind of a bad dream. I'd say we ought to hightail it out of here and get back home, only . . ."

"Only, if you did that, you'd never know the answer, would you?" said Jupiter. "I would suggest that you employ a firm of private investigators."

"Hey, we couldn't do that!" protested Tom. "We aren't wracked in poverty, but we aren't exactly rolling in the green stuff either. Private investigators cost money."

"You'll find this firm very reasonable," said Jupiter. He took a card out of his pocket and handed it to Tom. It was an oversized business card, and it read:

THE THREE INVESTIGATORS

"We Investigate Anything"

? ? ?

First Investigator .... Jupiter Jones
Second Investigator .... Pete Crenshaw
Records and Research .... Bob Andrews

Tom read the card and smiled a wry smile. "You're putting me on," he said.

"I am quite serious," Jupiter told him. "Our record is very impressive."

"Why the question marks?" asked Tom.

"I knew you would ask that," said Jupiter. "The question mark is the universal symbol of something unknown. The three question marks stand for The Three Investigators, and we are prepared to solve any mystery which may be brought to us. You might say that the question marks are our trademark."

Tom folded the card and tucked it into his shirt pocket. "Okay," he said. "So if The Three Investigators take on the case of the missing grandfather, what then?"

"First," said Jupiter, "I suggest that any agreement between us remain between us. Your mother is already somewhat upset. She might, quite unwittingly, disturb any arrangements we might make."

Tom nodded. "Grownups do gum things up," he said.

"Second, Officer Haines is right. I think it unwise that you and your mother remain in this house alone."

"You mean you want us to go back to the Seabreeze Inn?"

"It will depend upon your mother, of course," said Jupiter. "However, if you remain here, you would probably be more comfortable if one of the investigators stayed in the house with you."

"I don't know about Mom," said Tom, "but I'd be a darn sight happier."

"It's settled then," said Jupiter. "I'll talk it over with Bob and Pete."

"Jupiter!" Aunt Mathilda bustled out of the house. "We have finished putting up the other bed. I must say, you could have been a little more helpful."

"Sorry, Aunt Mathilda. Tom and I got to talking."

Aunt Mathilda sniffed. "I have been trying to persuade Mrs. Dobson to return to the inn, but she insists that she will remain here. She has the ridiculous idea that her father will show up at any moment."

"Perhaps he will," said Jupiter. "This is his home."

Mrs. Dobson came out, looking pale but somewhat braver after her cup of tea.

"Well, my dear," said Aunt Mathilda, "if there's nothing more we can do for you, we'll be going. If you get frightened, just call. And do be careful."

Eloise promised that she would be most careful, and that they would lock the house securely.

"They'll have to get a locksmith, you know," said Aunt Mathilda as she, Jupiter, and Hans drove down the road toward Rocky Beach. "They can lock the doors from the inside, but they can't unlock them from the outside. That crazy Potter must have all the keys with him. And they should have a telephone put in. It's simply madness for them to be there without a telephone."

Jupe agreed. When they reached the salvage

yard, he slipped away and crawled through Tunnel Two to call Pete Crenshaw and Bob Andrews.

"The Three Investigators have a client," he told Pete, "and this time, it is not Jupiter Jones!"

7

A Royal Tragedy

It was after five when The Three Investigators met in their trailer Headquarters. Jupiter reported briefly on the Dobsons' move to The Potter's house, and on the flaming footprints which had appeared in the kitchen.

"Good grief!" exclaimed Pete. "You don't suppose The Potter died, and is coming back to haunt the place?"

"That is what Hans suggested," said Jupiter. "But those footprints were not made by The Potter. At least, they were not The Potter's footprints. The Potter has gone barefoot for many years. You may have noticed that his feet have spread. The footprints were small; they might be the prints of a short man, or of a woman."

"Mrs. Dobson?" said Pete.

"She would not have had time to manage it," said Jupiter. "She went down the stairs and out to the truck to get the groceries. I followed immediately. She had already gotten the groceries and was about to enter the kitchen when she saw the flames. I was right behind her. Also, why would she do such a thing? And how was it accomplished?"

"The men from Hilltop House?" suggested Pete.

"A possibility," said Jupiter. "They came down to the beach as we started moving the Dobsons in. We have no assurance that they stayed on the beach. They could have walked in through the front door, which was open, set the footprints to flaming in some manner, and slipped out the back way and down to the beach again. Pete, what were you able to find out about Hilltop House?"

Pete took a small notebook out of his pocket. "Mr. Holtzer has never been so happy," he told the others. "I stopped in his office today to see if he wanted his lawn mowed—which he doesn't—and I didn't even have to ask any questions. He's had Hilltop House on his books for about fifteen years, and it's such a mouldering ruin that he's never been able to sell it or rent it or even give it away, and then along comes this man who decides it is the one and only house in Rocky Beach, and he has to have it. Took a year's lease and paid three months in advance. Mr. Holtzer had the lease out on his desk—I think he was figuring his commission—so I got a look at the new tenant's name."

"Which is?"

"Mr. Ilyan Demetrieff," said Pete. "Or maybe it's Demetrioff. I was looking at it upside down, and Mr. Holtzer needs to clean his typewriter. Anyhow, Demetrieff, or Demetrioff, listed his previous address as 2901 Wilshire Boulevard, Los Angeles."

Bob reached for the Central Telephone Directory which was on top of a file cabinet, leafed through, then shook his head. "He's not listed."

"Lots of people aren't," said Jupiter. "We can check the address later and see what we can find out about Mr. Demetrieff." Jupiter pulled at his lower lip. "I wish we knew more about the double-headed eagle. I think that may be very important. It appears not only on The Potter's medallion, and on those two urns in his yard, but there is an immense plaque in one of his bedrooms with the design. It seems to have fascinated The Potter."

Bob Andrews grinned. "On that we lucked out," he told Jupiter.

"What do you mean?"

"We don't have to wait for the library to open tomorrow," said Bob. "My father bought a coffee-table book."

"A what?" said Pete.

"A coffee-table book—one of those big picture books they're always advertising by mail. Dad's got a weakness for them." Bob had been sitting with a cardboard package at his feet. Now, smiling proudly, he put the package on the desk and opened it. Jupiter and Pete saw a handsome volume with a glossy jacket. *Royal Riches,* read the title. *A photographic study of the crown jewels of Europe, with commentary by E. P. Farnsworth.*

"Isn't that the British crown?" said Jupiter, looking at the magnificent object which decorated the cover. It had been photographed at close range, resting on a scarlet velvet cloth.

"One of them," said Bob. "The British have a couple of crowns, plus so many scepters and orbs and maces and swords you wouldn't believe it. The guys who did this book covered a lot of territory. They've got photographs of the British crown jewels, plus the crown of Charlemagne, which is in Austria, and the crown of St. Stephen of Hungary. Also something called the Lombard crown, which is made out of iron. There's a little bit on Russia, and the Russians went in for eagles in a big way, but I think the eagle we want is this one."

Bob had paged through past the middle of the book. He pushed the volume across the desk to Jupe. "The imperial crown of Lapathia," he said.

Pete bent over Jupe's shoulder to stare. "Yeah!" he exclaimed.

The imperial crown of Lapathia looked more like a helmet than a crown—but a helmet of gold, solidly encrusted with blue stones. At the top, four bands of gold encircled a huge ruby, and above this gem was an eagle—a scarlet eagle with two heads. The brilliant wings were spread wide, and the heads looked to right and to left, diamond eyes glittering, beaks open in fierce, warlike defiance.

"It certainly looks very much like The Potter's eagle," said Jupiter.

"The commentary is on the next page," said Bob.

Jupe turned the page and began to read aloud:

" 'The imperial crown of Lapathia was fashioned by the artisan Boris Kerenov in approximately 1543. Kerenov based his design for the crown on the helmet worn by Duke Federic Azimov in the battle of Karlon. Azimov's victory at Karlon brought to an end the civil wars which had devastated the tiny country of Lapathia. After their defeat by Azimov's army, the barons of the south each took a solemn oath that the peace of Lapathia would not again be broken. The following year, Duke Federic called the nobles to meet in the fortress of Madanhoff, and there he declared himself king of Lapathia. The nobles, isolated in the fortress and cut off from their own armies, bowed to the wishes of Duke Federic and pledged their allegiance to him as sovereign ruler. One dissenter, Ivan the Bold, refused to take the oath of allegiance. Legend has it that this proud warrior was executed in the main hall of Madanhoff, and his head was impaled on a spear and displayed on the battlements of the fortress.

" 'The coronation of Federic I of Lapathia took place in the chapel at Madanhoff in 1544. The crown, designed and executed by Kerenov, remained in the possession of the Azimov family for almost 400 years, and was last used in the coronation of William IV in 1913. Following the overthrow of the Azimov dynasty in 1925, the crown was declared the property of the people of Lapathia. It is now on display in the National Museum at Madanhoff, the capital city which grew up around the site of Duke Federic's ancient stronghold.

" 'The Azimov crown, solid gold and set with lapis lazuli, is surmounted by a huge ruby said to have been the possession of Ivan the Bold, whose estates were forfeited to Federic Azimov after his execution. The two-headed eagle atop the ruby is the family device of the Azimovs. Kerenov fashioned it of enamel on gold. The eyes are diamonds, each weighing more than two carats.' "

Jupiter stopped reading and turned back to examine the photograph of the crown again.

"That's one way to get to the top," said Pete. "Kill off the opposition."

"Swiping the poor guy's ruby and sticking it in the crown was a nasty touch," said Bob.

"They played rough back in those days," said Jupiter.

"They played rough in 1925, too," said Bob. He had his notebook out. "I looked up Lapathia in the encyclopedia. Believe it or not, it's still there."

"You mean none of the big powers gobbled it up?" said Jupe.

"No. It is now the Republic of Lapathia, area 73 square miles, with a population of about 20,000 people. The major industry is cheese. There is a standing army of 350 men, 35 of whom are generals."

"That's one general for every ten soldiers," exclaimed Pete.

"Well, you can't say they lack direction," laughed Jupe. "What else?"

"The National Assembly of Lapathia is the governing body, and is made up of the 35 generals plus one representative from each of the departments or provinces. There are ten provinces, so I guess we know how the voting goes."

"The generals run the country," said Jupiter.

"They also elect the president," said Bob.

"But what about the Azimovs?" asked Pete.

"Aha! They are *not* still there. I said they played rough in 1925. William IV—you remember, he was the last one to wear the crown—decided that the royal treasury was getting low. He had married a Lapathian lady—she was a cousin, actually, so she was an Azimov, too—and she had very expensive tastes. She liked diamond bracelets and Paris gowns and she also had four children, each of whom had to have his own tutor and his own carriage and his own horses. King William ran into debt, so he put a tax on every pound of cheese that came out of the Lapathian dairies. Naturally, the Lapathians were unhappy, and the generals saw their chance. They waited until King William's birthday, when all of the Azimovs would be gathered in the capital, and they marched into the palace and told William he wasn't going to be king anymore."

"What happened then?" asked Jupiter.

"Probably much the same thing that happened to old Ivan the Bold," said Bob. "The official account is that His Majesty became distraught and jumped off a balcony."

"Someone shoved him!" declared Pete, horrified.

"It seems likely," said Bob. "The rest of the family became so upset that they did away with themselves in various ways. The queen is supposed to have taken poison."

"You mean the people believed that?" cried Pete.

"With all those generals around, who was going to argue?" Bob retorted. "Also, the generals immediately removed the tax on cheese, which helped.

The royal palace became the National Museum, and the crown jewels were donated to the people, so everybody could enjoy them."

"And no one could wear them," put in Jupiter. "A fantastic story. On the other hand, a tax on tea had a great deal to do with our American Revolution, so perhaps it isn't so fantastic. And are there no Azimovs left?"

"I'll double-check it at the library tomorrow," promised Bob. "According to the encyclopedia, the family became extinct when King William jumped off that balcony."

Jupe brooded. "Tom Dobson said his grandfather came from Ukrainia. Suppose Tom is wrong? The Potter and that Azimov eagle seem to be old friends. I wonder if he could have had anything to do with that royal family."

"Or with the revolutionary generals," added Bob.

Pete shivered. "Whole families do not commit suicide," he said. "Remember what happened to the Romanovs in Russia."

"They were massacred," said Jupe.

"Right. And if The Potter had any part in that, I don't want to know him any better than I do already."

8

Worthington Comes Through

"I am sure," said Jupiter Jones firmly, "that whatever may have happened in the past, Tom Dobson
and his mother know only that The Potter makes
beautiful ceramics and that he is missing. Also that
somebody or something left flaming footprints in
his kitchen this afternoon. Mrs. Dobson is extremely upset, and Tom is not at all happy about
the situation. I suggested to Tom that one of The
Three Investigators might spend the night with the
Dobsons. They will feel safer, and one of us will be
on the scene if something unusual occurs. There is
another line of inquiry I would like to follow up
with Bob. Pete, could you call your mother and—"

"Not me!" cried Pete. "Listen, Jupe, somebody
could burn that house down with those flaming
footprints! And the windows upstairs are awfully
high. If you got shoved out of one of them, you
might not recover."

"You won't be alone," Jupiter reminded him.

"King William wasn't alone, either."

"Well, if you won't, you won't," said Jupiter
Jones. "I had hoped, though . . ."

Pete scowled savagely. "All right! All right! I'll

do it. I get all the keen assignments." And he picked up the telephone and dialed his home.

"Mom?" he said. "I'm with Jupiter. Can I stay over tonight?"

The boys waited.

"Yeah, all night," said Pete. "We're looking for something. It's a medallion. It's lost."

The telephone made worried noises.

"Jupe says his aunt won't mind," said Pete. And, "Yes, I'll be home early in the morning." And, "Yes, I know I'm supposed to cut the grass tomorrow."

Finally, "Okay, Mom. Thanks. See you." And Pete hung up.

"Beautiful!" said Bob.

"And quite true," announced Jupiter. "We are looking for a lost medallion—the one The Potter wears."

Then, at Jupiter's request, Bob called his mother and received permission to stay for supper with the Joneses.

"Jupiter!" Aunt Mathilda's voice carried clearly through the air vent in the top of the trailer. "Jupiter Jones! Where are you?"

"Just in time!" said Jupe. The boys hurried out as fast as they could through Tunnel Two, brushed off their knees, and emerged from Jupiter's outdoor workshop.

"I declare to Betsy!" exclaimed Aunt Mathilda, who stood near the office of the salvage yard. "I don't know what you boys do, puttering in that workshop all the time. Jupiter, supper's ready."

"Aunt Mathilda," said Jupe, "can Pete and Bob stay and . . ."

"Yes, they can stay and eat with us," said Aunt Mathilda. "We're only having pancakes and sausages, but there's plenty for everyone."

Pete and Bob thanked her and accepted the invitation.

"Call your folks," ordered Aunt Mathilda. "You can use the phone in the office. And lock up after yourselves. Five minutes, and I want you boys ready to eat."

She crossed the street to the house.

"Do you suppose she's a mind reader?" said Pete.

"I hope not," declared Jupiter fervently.

Five minutes later the boys were at the table in the Jones dining room, devouring pancakes and sizzling sausages, and listening to Uncle Titus tell of the old days, when Rocky Beach was only a wide spot in the road.

After supper, the boys leaped to help Aunt Mathilda clear away and do the dishes. When they had finished, and the sink was scoured to perfection, they made for the door.

"Where to now?" demanded Aunt Mathilda.

"We aren't quite finished with our job," Jupe explained.

"Well, don't be too late," warned Aunt Mathilda. "And don't leave the light on in the workshop. And remember to lock the gate again."

Jupiter promised that they would obey all instructions, and they escaped across the street, where Pete collected his bicycle.

"How will Tom Dobson know it's me?" Pete asked.

"Just tell him," Jupiter advised. "He has one of our cards."

"Okay." Pete wheeled out of the yard and started for the highway.

"Now to check on that Mr. Demetrieff who rented Hilltop House," Jupiter decided. "I think Worthington could help us there."

Some time before, Jupiter Jones had won a prize in a contest sponsored by the Rent-'n-Ride Auto Rental Company. The prize had been the use of a gold-plated Rolls-Royce and a chauffeur for thirty days. Worthington, the very proper English chauffeur who had driven Jupiter and his friends in the course of many of their investigations, had become a rather enthusiastic amateur sleuth himself, and always took an interest in the boys' cases.

Bob looked at his wristwatch. It was well past seven. "We can't ask Worthington to come out here this late," he said. "Not on a Sunday night."

"It won't be necessary to ask him to come here," said Jupiter. "Worthington lives in the Wilshire district. Unless he's terribly occupied with something, he could go and look at that address on Wilshire. Perhaps that would give us some clue to Mr. Demetrieff."

Bob agreed that this was worth a try, and the two boys crawled through Tunnel Two and back into

Headquarters, where Jupiter consulted his little telephone list and called Worthington's number.

"Master Jupiter?" Worthington sounded very pleased to hear Jupe's voice on the telephone. "How are you, sir?"

Jupiter assured Worthington that he was very well.

"I am afraid that the Rolls-Royce isn't available tonight," said Worthington ruefully. "There is a big party in Beverly Hills. Perkins took the car over."

"We didn't want the car tonight, Worthington," said Jupe. "I was only wondering if you would have time to do a small favor for The Three Investigators."

"I was busily engaged," said Worthington. "I was playing solitaire—and losing. The interruption is most welcome. What can I do for you?"

"We are attempting to get information on a Mr. Ilyan Demetrieff," Jupiter told him. He spelled the name for Worthington. "Possibly, it is Demetrioff, with an 'o,'" he told the chauffeur. "We are not positive. However, he has given his address as 2901 Wilshire Boulevard. We would like to know if Mr. Demetrieff has, in fact, recently lived at this address. Also, it would be interesting to know what kind of place 2901 Wilshire is."

"It's practically around the corner from me," said Worthington. "I shall stroll over and ring the bell."

"That's fine, Worthington," said Jupiter. "And what will you say if someone opens the door?"

Worthington scarcely hesitated. "I shall inform

them that I am chairman of the Volunteer Committee for the Beautification of Wilshire Boulevard," said Worthington. "I shall ask their opinion of putting potted shrubs along the sidewalks. If they are receptive to the idea, I can ask them to join the committee."

"Wonderful, Worthington!" cried Jupiter.

Worthington promised to call Headquarters within half an hour, and hung up briskly.

"There are times when I think we should take Worthington into our agency," laughed Jupiter after he reported the chauffeur's plan to Bob.

"He considers himself a member already," said Bob. "What do you think he'll find at that Wilshire address?"

"Possibly nothing," admitted Jupiter. "An empty house, or perhaps an apartment with no tenant. But at least he'll be able to tell us something about the neighborhood. I like the idea of a Volunteer Committee for the Beautification of Wilshire Boulevard. We could join the committee and ring doorbells in Mr. Demetrieff's area, and perhaps glean some information on Mr. Demetrieff."

"City people never know their neighbors," said Bob.

"Sometimes they know more than one thinks." Jupiter put his hands behind his head and leaned back in his chair. "Suppose it is a neighborhood of elderly people," he said. "Elderly people are home all day. They look out of their windows. They watch what is going on. I wonder how many crimes have been solved because some little old lady who slept lightly got up in the middle of the night to see who was making a noise on the street?"

Bob grinned. "Remind me to be careful when I go past Miss Hopper's."

"I think she doesn't miss a great deal," conceded Jupiter. He opened the book on the crown jewels which Bob had brought with him and stared at the photograph of the Azimov crown. "It is beautiful, in a barbaric way," he said. "I suppose it was typical of old Duke Federic to have it made in the shape of a helmet."

"He must have been a real charmer," said Bob. He shuddered. "Executing Ivan the Bold was bad enough. He didn't have to stick his head up on the castle wall."

"They did things like that in those days," said Jupe. "It was supposed to serve as an example, and I am sure it did. The Azimovs survived for 400 years afterward."

The telephone rang.

"That can't be the Wilshire Boulevard Beautification Committee already," exclaimed Bob. "He wouldn't have had time to do his stuff."

But it was Worthington. "I am sorry, Master Jupiter," the chauffeur reported, "but no one lives at 2901 Wilshire Boulevard. It is a small business building, and at this hour it is locked."

"Oh," said Jupiter.

"However, there was a light in the outer lobby, and I could read the building directory," Worthington announced brightly. "I made a list of the companies occupying the building. They are the

Acme Photostat Service, a Dr. H. H. Carmichael, the Jensen Secretarial Bureau, the Lapathian Board of Trade, Sherman Editorial—"

"Wait a minute!" cried Jupiter. "What was that last?"

"Sherman Editorial Bureau," said Worthington.

"No, the one before that? Did you say Lapathian—?"

"Lapathian Board of Trade," said Worthington.

"Worthington," declared Jupiter, "I think you have told us exactly what we want to know."

"I have?" Worthington sounded astonished. "There was no Mr. Demetrieff listed," he reminded Jupiter.

"Well, if you were to ask for him at the Lapathian Board of Trade," said Jupiter, "they might tell you that he's vacationing in Rocky Beach. Then again, they might not. Thanks, Worthington. And good night."

Jupiter put down the telephone. "Our new tenant at Hilltop House hails from the Lapathian Board of Trade," he told Bob. He looked again at the picture of the crown. "The scarlet eagle was the device of Lapathia, and a favorite symbol with The Potter. And a man from the Lapathian Board of Trade leases a house overlooking The Potter's shop. This suggests a number of interesting possibilities."

"Like The Potter is really a Lapathian?" said Bob.

"Also, that we might pay a visit to Hilltop House, tonight," said Jupe firmly.

9

Hilltop House

Bob and Jupe slipped out of The Jones Salvage Yard through Red Gate Rover and hurried toward the place where a hiking trail meandered in a series of switchbacks to the top of Coldwell Hill.

"We could take the coward's way out," said Bob, looking up toward the top of the hill. "We could take our bikes up to The Potter's and leave them there and walk up the lane to Hilltop House."

"That would scarcely be the coward's way out," said Jupiter. "We do not know what brought those two men to Hilltop House. I would prefer to approach the place without being seen. It is unlikely that they are watching the fire road, but they might easily spot us if we attempted to walk up their lane from the highway."

"You're right," admitted Bob. He turned to look back toward the sea. The sun had already disappeared behind a bank of fog that lurked offshore. "It'll be dark before we can get back here."

"We should have no difficulty," said Jupiter Jones. "The moon will be up shortly."

"You checked the almanac?" asked Bob.

"I checked the almanac."

"Silly of me to ask," said Bob, and he started up the trail. Jupiter followed more slowly, panting as the going got steep, and stopping now and then to rest. But after ten minutes he had his second wind and climbed more easily. Finally, "Here it is," said Bob.

He turned and held out a hand to Jupe to help him up onto the fire road that ran along the crest of the hill. "It'll be a snap from here," he said. "We'll be on a downgrade all the way to Hilltop House."

Jupe stood for a few seconds, looking north along the fire road. It was almost dark and the moon was not yet up. Still, the road—almost eight feet of bare earth scraped clear of growth—looked like a tawny ribbon stretching along the top of the range of hills. The scrub oak that crowded close to its sandy surface seemed black and menacing in the fading light.

"What do you expect to find tonight?" questioned Bob.

"Most certainly the two strangers who stopped at the salvage yard," said Jupiter. "One of them, we assume, is Mr. Demetrieff of the Lapathian Board of Trade. The other could be almost anyone. It will be interesting to see how they are amusing themselves at Hilltop House."

Jupiter began to walk, and Bob stepped briskly along beside him. The moon edged up beyond the hills, silvering the road and throwing deep black shadows beside the boys. There was little conversation until the hulking, dark mass of Hilltop House came into sight ahead and to their left. The upper stories of the place were dark, but a light gleamed faintly in one of the lower rooms.

"I explored that house once," said Bob. "I think that light is in what used to be the library."

"Windows could use a cleaning," murmured Jupiter, "and that does not look like an electric lamp."

"No. More like a lantern or a kerosene lamp. Well, give them a chance. They just moved in yesterday."

A little stream bed ran down the hill from the fire road and curved past Hilltop House. It was summer-dry now, and the boys stepped into it silently, feeling step by step for any loose pebbles which might slide and send them tumbling. They almost crawled for the last fifty feet before the wash turned and ran beside the retaining wall that held the driveway of Hilltop House firm.

Jupiter pulled himself up over the retaining wall and onto a paved apron at the rear of the house. The big Cadillac stood outside a triple garage. Jupiter walked once around the car, saw that it was empty, and decided to ignore it.

The windows that looked out onto the rear area were black. There was a door with a pane of glass set into the upper half, and it was locked. "Kitchen," decided Jupiter.

"The servants' quarters are upstairs," said Bob.

"They have hardly had time to acquire servants," said Jupiter. "I suggest we proceed directly to the library."

"Jupe! You're not planning on going inside?" Bob's voice came in a horrified whisper.

"I think not," said Jupe. "It might lead to unnecessary unpleasantness. We can go around the house and look into the library window."

"Okay," said Bob. "Just so long as we stay outside. If anything goes wrong, we can run like crazy."

Jupiter didn't answer this. He led the way around past the dark kitchen to the lighted windows of the library. There was a narrow, paved path which made the going easy. The shrubbery that had once decorated the side of the house had long since withered away from neglect and lack of water.

The library windows, as Jupiter had pointed out, could have used a good cleaning. The boys knelt and peered in over the sill and saw, mistily, the two strangers who had stopped at the salvage yard the day before. Two cots had been set up in the huge room. Cans and paper plates and paper napkins were heaped helter-skelter on shelves which had once held books. There was a fire roaring away in the fireplace, and the younger man—the driver of the Cadillac—knelt in front of the flames and toasted a hot dog on a long piece of wire. The ageless, hairless man sat in a folding chair at a card table. He had the air of a man waiting in a restaurant for the waiter to serve his dinner.

Bob and Jupe watched the younger man turn the hot dog on the improvised spit. Then the bald man made an impatient movement, got up, and walked away through the wide arch into a darkened room beyond the library. He was gone for some minutes, and when he returned the hot dog was ready. The younger man inserted it clumsily into a roll, put it on a paper plate, and placed it before the bald man.

Jupiter could hardly suppress a chuckle at the expression of the bald one as he confronted his hot dog. He had seen Aunt Mathilda look like that once when a Danish friend in Rocky Beach had served cold eels and scrambled eggs at a dinner party.

The boys backed away from the window and returned to the rear of the house.

Bob leaned on the Cadillac. "Now we know what they're doing," he said. "That's the untidiest camp-out I ever saw."

"There has to be more to it than that," declared Jupiter. "No one would rent a mansion—however aged—so that they could sleep on cots and toast hot dogs in the library. Where did that bald man go when he walked through the archway?"

"The living room's on the ocean side of the house," said Bob.

"And the terrace," Jupiter reminded him. "Come on."

Bob followed Jupiter to the corner of the house. The terrace adjoined the drive, and extended all the way across the front of the place. It was almost fifteen feet wide, made of smoothly poured cement and edged with a stone wall more than three feet high.

"There's something set up there," whispered Jupiter. "An instrument of some kind, on a tripod."

"A telescope?" said Bob.

"Probably. Listen!"

A man's voice came to them where they stood. Jupiter pressed himself close to the house, watching. The younger man came out of the house onto the moonlit terrace, crossed to the instrument on the tripod, looked into it, then called out something. He looked again and laughed, then made another remark. Jupiter frowned. The cadence of the speech was peculiar. There was almost a singsong quality to what the man said.

Then a second, deeper voice was heard. It was a voice which sounded immensely tired. The bald man stepped out onto the terrace, came to the tripod and bent to peer into it. He said a word or two, shrugged, and returned to the house. The younger man hurried after him, speaking rapidly and urgently.

"Not French," said Jupiter when they had gone.

"Or German," said Bob, who had had a year of that language.

"I wonder," said Jupiter, "what Lapathian sounds like."

"I wonder," said Bob, "what they were looking at."

"That, at least, we can find out," said Jupiter. He stepped quickly and noiselessly from the drive onto the terrace and stole forward to the instrument on its tripod. As Bob had guessed, the thing was a telescope. Jupiter bent, careful not to touch the instrument, and looked through the lens.

He saw the back windows of The Potter's house. The bedrooms were brightly lighted, and he could clearly see Pete sitting on a bed, talking with young Tom Dobson. There was a checker board between the two boys. Tom jumped one of Pete's men, and Pete made a wry face and pondered his next move. Mrs. Dobson came into the room carrying a tray on which there were three cups. Cocoa, Jupiter assumed.

Jupiter stepped away from the telescope and returned to the driveway. "We now know how they are amusing themselves," he told Bob. "They are spying on The Potter's house."

"About what you expected," said Bob. "Let's get out of here, Jupe. Those two give me the willies."

"Yes. And there is nothing more to be learned at the moment," said Jupiter Jones.

The boys passed the Cadillac and headed for the retaining wall to let themselves down again into the dry stream bed.

"It's closer here, I think," said Bob, cutting across an open patch of ground which might once have been a kitchen garden.

And with that, Bob suddenly shouted, threw up his arms, and dropped out of sight.

10

Caught!

"Bob, are you hurt?"

Jupiter knelt beside the hole which had appeared in the earth. Below, in what seemed to be some sort of cellar, Jupe could barely see Bob getting to his knees.

"Blast!" said Bob.

"Are you hurt?"

Bob stood up and hunched his shoulders. "No, I don't think so."

Jupiter stretched full length on the ground and reached one hand toward Bob. "Here!" he said.

Bob grasped the hand, put one foot on a shelf and tried to climb out of the hole. Wood splintered under his feet and he fell back, almost taking Jupe with him.

"Blast!" he said again, and then he froze, caught by the sudden beam of a very powerful flashlight.

"Do not move!" said the younger of the two tenants of Hilltop House.

Jupiter did not move, and Bob remained where he was, sitting on bare earth at the bottom of the hole, staring up past rotted, splintered planks.

"Exactly what are you doing here?" demanded the younger resident of Hilltop House.

Only Jupiter Jones could manage an air of superiority while stretched full-length on the ground. "At this precise moment," he said, "I was endeavoring to get my friend out of this hole. Please assist me, so that we can ascertain as quickly as possible whether he is injured."

"Why you impudent—!" began the younger man.

This outburst was interrupted by a deep chuckle. "Peace, Demetrieff," said the older, bald person. He knelt, surprisingly agile for one who was not slender, and reached toward Bob. "Can you take my hand?" he asked Bob. "We do not have a ladder on the premises."

Bob stood up and stretched, and in a second the bald man had hauled him up through the jagged hole and set him upon his feet. "Now how does it go?" he asked. "No bones broken, eh? Good. Nasty things, broken bones. I remember the time my horse fell on me. It was two months before I could ride again. It is painful when one must lie still and do nothing." The bald one paused, then added in a cold voice, "Naturally, I shot the horse."

Bob swallowed, and Jupiter felt goose bumps come up on his arms.

"Klas Kaluk is not noted for his patience with bunglers," said the younger man.

Jupiter stood up slowly, brushing dust from his clothes.

"Klas Kaluk?" he echoed.

"You would say General Kaluk," the younger man informed him. Jupiter was suddenly aware

that the younger man held a gun as well as a flashlight.

"General Kaluk." Jupiter nodded to the bald one, then turned back to the man with the gun. "And you are Mr. Demetrieff," he said.

"How did you know that?" demanded Demetrieff.

"General Kaluk called you by name," said Jupiter.

The general chuckled again. "You have a quick ear, my plump friend," he told Jupiter. "Boys with quick ears interest me. They hear many things. Shall we go into the house and discuss what you may have heard tonight?"

"Hey, Jupe," said Bob quickly. "Hey, we don't really want to. I mean, I'm okay, and we can go now and . . ."

The man named Demetrieff made a quick motion with his gun and Bob fell silent.

"It would be most inadvisable for us to leave this gaping hole in your yard," said Jupiter. "Some other member of the Chaparral Walking Club might cut across this way and fall in. Would you be liable, Mr. Demetrieff, or would it be General Kaluk?"

Again the bald general laughed. "You have a nimble set of wits, my friend," he told Jupiter. "I believe, however, that the owners of this house would be liable. However, as I said, broken bones are unpleasant things. Demetrieff, there are some planks behind the stable."

"I think it's a garage," ventured Bob.

"No matter. Get them and put them over the hole." The older man looked down through the gap at broken shelves and earth floor. "It seems that we have an extension to the foundation of this building which projects out under the garden. A wine cellar, I should think."

Demetrieff hauled a pair of damp and dirty two-by-fours from behind the garage and dropped them hastily into place across the hole.

"That should take care of the matter, at least for the moment," said General Kaluk. "Now we shall go into the house and you will tell me about this Chaparral Walking Club of yours. You will also tell me your names, and why you chose to walk across this piece of property."

"We would be delighted," said Jupiter.

The man named Demetrieff gestured toward the kitchen door, and General Kaluk led the way. Jupe and Bob trailed after the general. They went through a dusty and disused kitchen to the library, where the general sat easily in the folding chair next to the card table and ordered Jupiter and Bob to sit on one of the folding cots in the room.

"We cannot offer you lavish hospitality," said the general. His bald head gleamed in the light from the fireplace. "A glass of hot tea, perhaps?"

Jupiter shook his head. "Thank you, sir. I don't drink tea."

"Me, either," said Bob.

"Oh, yes," said the general. "I forget. There is

some custom about American children, is there not? No tea or coffee—or wine. You drink milk, do you?"

Jupiter admitted it.

"Well, we have no milk," said the general. Demetrieff stood to one side, a little behind the general.

"Demetrieff, have you heard of this Chaparral Walking Club?" asked the general.

"Never," said Demetrieff.

"It's a local thing," said Jupiter quickly. "Walking in the chaparral is more pleasant by day, but sometimes hikers try the fire roads on fine nights like this. You can hear the animals stirring in the underbrush as you pass. Sometimes, if you stand still for a long time, you can see the animals. I saw a deer once, and several times a skunk has crossed the road in front of me."

"Fascinating," said the man named Demetrieff. "And I suppose you also watch birds."

"Not at night," declared Jupiter truthfully. "You do hear an owl occasionally, but you never see one. In the daytime, the chaparral is alive with birds, but—"

The general held up one hand. "A moment," he said. "Chaparral. This is a new word. Will you explain to me, please, what it is?"

"It's a community of growing things," said Jupiter. "The plants you see on this hillside are all part of the chaparral community—they are dwarfed trees and shrubs—the scrub oak and juniper and the sage, and at higher elevations the manzanita.

They are extremely hardy plants which can survive
on very little rainfall. California is one of the few
areas where chaparral exists, so there is great interest in the plants."

Bob sat silently and marveled at Jupiter's almost
total recall of an article on chaparral that had appeared in a recent issue of *Nature* magazine. Total
recall, Bob knew, was not uncommon among ac-
tors who had to remember lines, and Jupiter had
once been a child actor.

On went Jupiter Jones, and on and on, describ-
ing the smell of chaparral in the spring, after the
rains. He was telling how it held the hillsides firm
when General Kaluk suddenly lifted one hand.

"Enough," said the general. "I share your admiration for chaparral. Courageous plants, if plants
can be said to have courage. Now, if you please, we
will get to the point. Your names?"

"Jupiter Jones," said Jupe.

"Bob Andrews," said Bob.

"Very well. And now you will tell me what you
were doing in my garden."

"It's a shortcut," said Jupe truthfully. "We hiked
up the fire road from Rocky Beach and cut across.
We can get down to the highway on your lane."

"The lane is private property."

"Yes, sir. We know. But Hilltop House has been
empty for many years, and people have become accustomed to using the lane when they hike."

"They will have to become unaccustomed," declared the general. "I think, Jupiter Jones, that I
have met you before."

"We didn't actually meet," said Jupe. "Mr. Demetrieff talked to me yesterday when you took the wrong turn off the highway."

"Ah, yes. And with you was an elderly man with a beard. Who is he?"

"We call him The Potter," said Jupiter. "I believe that is his real name—Alexander Potter."

"He is a friend of yours?" asked the general.

"I know him," admitted Jupiter. "Everyone in Rocky Beach knows The Potter."

The general nodded. "I believe I have heard of him." He turned toward Demetrieff, and firelight gleamed on his tanned skin. Jupiter saw a fine tracery of wrinkles on his cheeks. Kaluk was not ageless; he was old.

"Demetrieff," said the general, "did you not tell me there was a famed craftsman here who made pots?"

"And other things," put in Bob.

"I would enjoy very much meeting him," said the general. It was not exactly a question, and yet the general paused as if he were waiting for a reply.

Neither Jupiter nor Bob said anything.

"It is his shop at the bottom of my hill," said the general at last.

"It is his shop," said Jupiter.

"And he has guests," the general went on. "A young woman and a boy. Unless I make a mistake, you helped them today when they arrived at the shop."

"That's right," said Jupiter.

"A neighborly thing to do, no doubt," said the general. "You know those people?"

"No, sir," said Jupiter. "They're friends of Mr. Potter from someplace in the Midwest."

"Friends," said the general. "How pleasant to have friends. One would think this man who makes pots—and other things—would be present to greet his friends."

"He's . . . uh . . . rather eccentric."

"One gathers this. Yes, I would like very much to meet him. In fact, I must insist upon it."

The general suddenly sat straight, gripping the arms of his chair. "Where is he?" he demanded.

"Huh?" said Bob.

"You heard me. Where is the man you call The Potter?"

"We don't know," Jupiter said.

"That is impossible!" said the general. A flush of color rose to his leathery cheeks. "He was with you yesterday. Today you helped his friends when they arrived at his house. You know where he is!"

"No, sir," said Jupiter. "We have no idea where he went after he left the salvage yard yesterday."

"He sent you here!" The accusation was curt.

"No!" cried Bob.

"Do not tell me fairy tales about wandering in the chaparral!" shouted the general. He beckoned to his associate. "Demetrieff! Your gun, if you please!"

The man handed the weapon to the general.

"You know what to do," said Kaluk harshly.

Demetrieff nodded and began to unbuckle his belt.

"Hey, wait a minute!" shouted Bob.

"You will remain seated," said General Kaluk. "Demetrieff, take the fat one who talks so well. I want to hear him talk more."

Demetrieff went around behind the cot on which Jupe and Bob were seated. Jupiter felt the leather of the belt settle around his head.

"Now you will tell me about The Potter," said the general. "Where is he?"

The belt tightened on Jupiter's head.

"I don't know," said Jupiter.

"He simply walked away from your . . . your salvage yard and was not seen again?" The general was almost sneering.

"That's what happened."

The belt tightened some more.

"And he was expecting guests—these friends you speak of—these friends to whom you were so helpful."

"That's right."

"And your police have done nothing?" demanded Kaluk. "They have not looked for this man who walked away?"

"It's a free country," said Jupiter. "If The Potter chooses to walk away, he is entitled to do so."

"A free country?" The general blinked and ran a hand over his hairless chin. "Yes. Yes, I have heard that before. He said nothing to you? You swear it?"

"He said nothing," declared Jupiter. He stared straight at the general, unblinking.

"I see." The general stood up and walked to Jupiter. He looked at him for half a minute, then sighed. "Very well, Demetrieff. We will let them go. He is telling the truth."

The younger man protested. "It's mad! Too much of a coincidence!"

The general shrugged. "A pair of children, curious as all children are curious. They know nothing."

The belt was removed from Jupiter's head. Bob, who had not realized that he was holding his breath, let out a great gasp of relief.

"We should call your excellent police, who do not look for people," snapped Demetrieff. "We should tell them that you have broken the law. You have trespassed on this property."

"You talk about breaking the law!" exclaimed Bob. "If we told what happened here tonight . . ."

"You will not tell," said the general. "What really happened tonight? I asked about a famous artisan, and you informed me that you did not know his whereabouts. What could be more natural? The man has achieved some fame. He has been written about in your periodicals. As for this"—the general tossed the gun in his hand—"as for this, Mr. Demetrieff has a permit for the gun, and you *were* trespassing. Nothing has occurred. We are being generous. You may go now, and do not return."

Bob was up instantly, pulling Jupiter along with him.

"You will find it convenient to use the lane," said

the general. "And remember, we will be watching you go."

The boys did not speak until they were away from the house and hurrying down the drive that led from Hilltop House to the highway.

"Never again!" exclaimed Bob.

Jupiter looked up and back at the stone buttress of the terrace. Demetrieff and the general stood there, plain in the moonlight, motionless and watching.

"Malignant pair," said Jupiter. "I have a distinct feeling that General Kaluk has presided over other inquisitions."

"If you mean he's used to giving the third degree to people, I couldn't agree more," said Bob. "Nice that you have an honest face."

"It was even nicer to be able to tell the truth," said Jupiter.

"Yeah! You did that, didn't you?"

"I tried. One can consider one's daughter a friend from the Midwest."

The road curved then, and Hilltop House was lost to sight behind a clump of brush on the boys' left. And then, from lower on the hill, there was a muffled sound and a flash of flame. Something, or some things, whizzed over Bob's head and spattered into the brush.

"Get down!" cried Jupiter.

Bob dropped on his face, Jupe beside him. The two waited, not daring to move. There was a crackling in the underbrush off to the right. Then there was quiet, except for the scolding of some night bird.

"Buckshot?" wondered Bob.

"I think so," Jupiter decided. He got to his hands and knees and crawled forward until they had rounded yet another turn in the lane. Bob followed him. When they had gone perhaps fifty yards in this fashion, both boys leaped up and sprinted for the highway.

The gate at the bottom of the drive was closed. They did not pause to see whether the lock was in place. Jupe climbed over and Bob hurdled the barrier in one leap. The two raced down the road to The Potter's gate and burst through that, stopping only when they had reached the shelter of The Potter's front porch.

"That shot!" gasped Jupiter. "It couldn't have come from Hilltop House. Demetrieff and the general were standing on the terrace there as we came around the bend in the road." He stopped to let his breathing quiet. Then, "Someone was waiting on the hill with a gun. Bob, there's a third man involved!"

11

The Ghost Returns

Jupiter Jones had his hand on the doorbell of The Potter's house when a window upstairs was thrown open and Eloise Dobson's voice called out.

"Who's there?" Mrs. Dobson demanded.

Jupiter stepped back away from the door and out from under the roof of the porch. "It's Jupiter Jones, Mrs. Dobson. And Bob Andrews is with me."

"Oh," said Mrs. Dobson. "Just a second."

The window slammed shut. An instant later, Jupe and Bob heard locks turning and bolts being drawn back. The door opened and Pete looked out.

"What's up?" he demanded.

"Let us in, and keep calm," said Jupiter in a low voice.

"I am calm. What's the matter?"

Jupe and Bob stepped into the hall. "I don't want to alarm Mrs. Dobson unnecessarily," said Jupiter quickly, "but the men at Hilltop House—"

Jupiter broke off when Mrs. Dobson appeared at the top of the stairs and started down. "Did you hear a loud bang a minute ago, Jupiter?" she asked. "Like a shot?"

"It was only a backfire on the highway," said Jupiter quickly. "Mrs. Dobson, you haven't met our friend, Bob Andrews."

"How do you do, Mrs. Dobson," said Bob.

Mrs. Dobson smiled and came the rest of the way down the stairs. "I'm glad to meet you, Bob," she said. "What brings you two here so late?"

Tom Dobson came down the stairs carrying a tray piled with empty cups. "Hey, Jupe!" he said.

Again Jupiter introduced Bob.

"Aha!" said Tom. "The Third Investigator!"

"The what?" said Mrs. Dobson.

"Nothing, Mom," said Tom. "It's just a joke. Kind of."

"Hm!" Mrs. Dobson looked at her son in the searching manner peculiar to mothers. "We can do without jokes right now," she said. "What are you boys up to? It's not that I don't appreciate your trouble. It's very nice to have Pete spend the night with us, but let's not have any secrets, huh?"

"I'm sorry, Mrs. Dobson," said Jupiter. "Bob and I hadn't planned to come here tonight. However, we went hiking along the fire road at the top of the hill, and we could not help but notice the men at Hilltop House."

Bob choked.

Jupiter continued calmly. "Hilltop House is the big place almost directly behind this house, but up near the crest of the hill. Two new tenants moved into the place yesterday, and from their terrace they can look directly into the back bedrooms in this house. The thought came to us that you would wish to know of this, so that you can keep the window shades down."

"Oh, keen!" Mrs. Dobson sat down on the stairs. "Makes the day perfect. First we get flaming footprints, then that nut from the inn, and now a couple of Peeping Toms."

"Nut from the inn?" questioned Bob. "What nut, from what inn?"

"Guy named Farrier," answered Pete. "He popped up about half an hour ago, said he wanted to see if Mrs. Dobson and Tom got moved in okay, and was there anything he could do for them?"

"The jolly fisherman," said Jupiter.

"Too jolly for words," said Mrs. Dobson. "For some reason, he gives me the creeps. Why's he trying so hard? He smiles so much my face aches just watching him, and he's always so darned . . . so darned . . ."

"Splendid?" said Jupiter.

"I guess you could say splendid." Mrs. Dobson put her chin in her hands and rested her elbows on her knees. "He looks like . . . well, like one of those dummies in a department store. I don't think he sweats. Anyhow, he tried to invite himself in for coffee. I told him I was planning to lie down with a cold cloth on my head, and he took the hint and went away."

"He was driving?" said Jupiter.

"Well, sure," Pete put in. "An old tan Ford. He went on up the highway."

"Hm," said Jupiter. "No reason why he

shouldn't take a drive along the ocean. Well, we had better get home. See you tomorrow, Mrs. Dobson."

"Goodnight, boys," said Mrs. Dobson. She took the tray of dirty cups from Tom and headed for the kitchen.

Jupiter quickly filled in Tom and Pete on the full events at Hilltop House and the subsequent gunshot. He warned them again about keeping the shades down. After Jupe and Bob went out, they could hear the sound of locks being locked and bolts being bolted.

"I think I am extremely pleased that The Potter equipped his house so well with locks," said Jupiter.

The boys began the walk back to Rocky Beach on the shoulder of the highway.

"Do you think Pete and the Dobsons are in any real danger?" wondered Bob.

"No," said Jupiter. "No, I think not. The men at Hilltop House may be curious about them, but we know now that they are really interested in The Potter. And they are aware that The Potter is not at home."

"What about the guy on the hill?" said Bob. "You know, the one who took a shot at us."

"We were the ones who were threatened," said Jupiter. "It does not appear that he menaced the Dobsons in any way. It is interesting that Mr. Farrier has been so persistent in his attentions to Mrs. Dobson. She has certainly not encouraged him, and Aunt Mathilda was positively rude to him this afternoon. Most people do not intrude when they are clearly unwelcome. That tan Ford is also interesting."

"There must be a million of those around," said Bob. "Why is it interesting?"

"Because it doesn't match the rest of the man," explained Jupiter. "As Mrs. Dobson agreed, he is quite splendid in his appearance. One would expect him to drive something more elegant—a foreign sports car, perhaps. And although he seems meticulous about his own appearance, he has not even troubled to have his car washed."

The lights of Rocky Beach gleamed ahead, and the boys walked faster, suddenly fearful that Aunt Mathilda might be looking for them. The Jones house was quiet, however, when the boys reached it. Jupiter peered in through the window to see his Uncle Titus still napping contentedly as an old movie unfolded on the TV screen.

"Come over with me, and we'll close the yard up for the night," said Jupiter to Bob.

The boys went across and in through the big iron gates. The light burned brightly in Jupiter's outdoor workshop. As Jupiter reached to turn it off, a red light over the printing press flashed furiously off and on. This was the signal that the telephone in Headquarters was ringing.

"At this hour?" exclaimed Bob. "Now who—?"

"Pete!" said Jupiter. "It could only be Pete." He tore aside the grating that covered Tunnel Two. In seconds he and Bob were inside Headquarters and Jupiter had snatched up the telephone.

"Come back!" Pete's voice sounded thin and shaky coming over the wire. "It's happened again!"

"More footprints?" said Jupiter tersely.

"Three of them, on the stairs," said Pete. "I put them out. There's a funny smell. Also, Mrs. Dobson is having hysterics."

"We'll be right there," promised Jupiter.

He hung up the telephone.

"Another set of flaming footprints," he told Bob. "On the stairs, this time. Also, Pete reports that Mrs. Dobson is having hysterics, which is not surprising."

"Back we go?" questioned Bob.

"Back we go," said Jupiter.

The boys hurried out through Tunnel Two and were just locking the gate of the salvage yard when Aunt Mathilda opened the door of the Jones house. "What are you boys doing over there all this time?" she called.

"Just sorting things out," Jupiter called back. He turned away from the gate and ran across to his aunt. "We thought we might ride up and see how Mrs. Dobson and Tom are getting along," he said. "Do you mind?"

"I do," said Aunt Mathilda. "It's too late to go visiting. And Jupiter, you know I don't like to have you on that highway after dark."

"The bikes have lights," Jupiter pointed out, "and we'll be careful. Mrs. Dobson was so upset this afternoon, we thought we might just check in on her and see if she's settled comfortably."

"Well . . . all right, Jupiter. But you boys be

careful." She stopped suddenly. "Where's Pete?" she asked.

"He left," said Jupiter shortly.

"All right. Well, if you're going, hurry. It's not getting any earlier. And remember—careful!"

"We'll remember," promised Jupiter.

With the bicycles, the return trip to The Potter's house took only minutes. Bob and Jupiter pounded on the front door and called, and Pete let them in.

"Did you search the house?" Jupiter asked.

"By myself?" said Pete. "You crazy? Besides, I've been busy. I had a set of burning footprints to put out, and a trip to the telephone on the highway to call you guys, and Mrs. Dobson is way out in left field."

Indeed, Mrs. Dobson was not herself. Bob and Jupiter followed Pete upstairs to the big front bedroom where the brass bed had been put up. Mrs. Dobson was stretched out on the bed, face down, and sobbing bitterly. Young Tom Dobson sat beside her, patting her shoulder and looking highly nervous.

Bob slipped into the bathroom, turned on the cold water tap, and soaked a washcloth.

"There it goes again!" cried Mrs. Dobson.

"There what goes?" asked Jupiter.

"It stopped," said Mrs. Dobson. "The water was running someplace."

"I did that, Mrs. Dobson." Bob came in, carrying the wet cloth. "I thought you might use this."

"Oh." She took the cloth and swabbed at her face.

"Just after you left," Pete explained, "we could hear water running in the pipes, but every tap in the house was turned off. Then, we were all about to turn in, and there was this sound downstairs, like a thud. Mrs. Dobson came out to see what was up, and there were three little fires on the stairs. I smothered them with a blanket, and we've got another set of footprints."

Jupiter and Bob returned to the stairs to examine the charred marks.

"Exactly like the ones in the kitchen," said Jupiter. He touched one, then sniffed his fingertips. "Peculiar odor. Chemicals of some type."

"So what does that get us?" demanded Pete. "We've got a ghost with a Ph.D. in chemistry?"

"It is probably too late," said Jupiter, "but I suggest that we search the house."

"Jupe, nobody could have gotten in here," insisted Pete. "This place is locked up tighter than the vault at the Bank of America."

Jupiter insisted, however, and the house was searched from cellar to attic. Except for the Dobsons, The Three Investigators, and a vast amount of ceramic art, the place was empty.

"I want to go home," said Eloise Dobson.

"We'll go, Mom," promised Tom. "We'll go in the morning, okay?"

"What's the matter with right now?" asked Mrs. Dobson.

"You're tired, Mom."

"You think I could sleep in this place?" demanded Mrs. Dobson.

"Would you feel safer if we all stayed tonight?" asked Jupiter Jones.

Eloise Dobson shivered and stretched out on the brass bed, kicking at the footboard with her stocking feet. "I'd feel safer," she admitted. "Do you suppose we could ask the fire department up for the night, too?"

"Let's hope we don't need them," said Jupiter.

"Try to rest, huh, Mom?" Tom had padded out to the linen closet for an extra blanket. He covered his mother, who was still wearing the blouse and skirt she had had on that afternoon.

"I ought to get up and get undressed," said Mrs. Dobson wearily. She didn't, however. She put one arm up to cover her eyes. "Don't turn out the light," she said.

"I won't," said Tom.

"And don't go away," she murmured.

"I'll stay right here," said Tom.

Mrs. Dobson said nothing more. She had dropped into an exhausted slumber.

The boys tiptoed out to the landing. "I'll get another blanket and sleep on the floor in Mom's room," said Tom softly. "Will you guys really stay all night?"

"I can telephone Aunt Mathilda," announced Jupiter. "I will inform her that your mother is feeling rather upset and wishes company. And perhaps she can call Mrs. Andrews."

"I'll call my mother," said Bob. "I can just tell her I'm staying over with you."

"Maybe we should call the police," said Tom.

"So far that has done no good," Jupiter told him. "Lock the door after us when we go to the call box."

"Don't worry," said Pete.

"I'll rap three times when we come back," said Jupiter. "Then I'll wait, and rap three more times."

"Got you." Pete unlocked and unbolted the door and Jupiter and Bob slipped out into the night, crossed The Potter's yard, and went into the call box on the highway.

Aunt Mathilda was more than concerned when she learned that Mrs. Dobson was upset and wanted company. Jupiter did not mention the second set of flaming footprints to her. He spent the better part of his three minutes persuading her not to rouse Uncle Titus and have him come with the truck to collect the Dobsons and remove them bodily to the security and comfort of the Jones house. "Mrs. Dobson's asleep now," Jupiter said finally. "She only said she'd feel safer if we all stayed in the house with her."

"There aren't enough beds," argued Aunt Mathilda.

"We'll make do," said Jupiter. "It'll be all right."

Aunt Mathilda finally subsided and Jupiter gave the telephone to Bob, who simply received permission from his mother to spend the night with Jupiter.

The boys went back to The Potter's house, rapped the agreed-upon raps, and were admitted by Pete.

As Aunt Mathilda had pointed out, there were

not enough beds to go around—not even with Tom
Dobson sleeping on the floor in his mother's room.
Pete did not see this as an obstacle. One of them,
he decided, should be on watch at all times. Two
would sleep. They could take turns. Bob and Jupiter both felt that sentinel duty might be an excellent idea, and Jupe volunteered for the first watch
—which was to be for three hours. Bob disappeared into The Potter's bedroom, to stretch out on
The Potter's narrow, immaculate cot. Pete vanished
into the room which had been prepared for Tom.

Jupe stationed himself in the hall at the head of
the stairs. He sat down on the floor, leaned back
against the wall, and stared speculatively at the
charred marks on the steps—the marks of bare feet.
He sniffed at his own fingers. The chemical smell
which he had noticed when he first touched the
footprints was gone. Doubtless some extremely vol-
atile mixture had been used to create the flames.
Jupe wondered idly what it had been, then decided
that the substance itself wasn't important. What
was important was that someone had come into a
locked and double-locked house to create the eerie
and terrifying effect. How had it been done? And
by whom?

Of one thing Jupiter Jones was sure. No ghost
was playing a devilish prank. Jupiter Jones refused
to believe in ghosts.

12

The Secret Library

Jupiter awakened in Tom Dobson's bed and heard a determined clanking and slamming and clattering from the kitchen below. He groaned slightly, turned over, and looked at his watch. It was after seven.

"You awake?" Bob Andrews was looking in through the doorway.

"I am now." Jupiter got up slowly.

"Mrs. Dobson's furious," reported Bob. "She's down cooking breakfast."

"That's good. I could use breakfast. What's she furious about? Last night she only wanted to go home."

"Not this morning. This morning she's ready to take the town of Rocky Beach apart. Wonderful what a good night's sleep will do for a person. Come on down. You'll enjoy it. Reminds me of your Aunt Mathilda in one of her more active moods."

Jupiter chuckled, went into the bathroom and splashed some water on his face, put on his shoes—which were all he had bothered to remove the night before—and followed Bob down to the kitchen.

Pete and Tom were already sitting there watching as Eloise Dobson dealt with skillet and eggs. She was relieving herself of numerous opinions about The Potter, the house, the flaming footprints, and the ingratitude of a father who disappeared when his only daughter had taken the trouble to drive almost all the way across the country to see him.

"And don't think I'm going to let him get away with it," said Mrs. Dobson. "I'm not. I'm going down to the police station this morning and file a missing persons report on him, and then they'll have to look for him."

"Will that do any good, Mrs. Dobson?" Jupiter questioned. "If The Potter is missing because he wishes to be missing, it's difficult to see—"

"I don't wish him to be missing," interrupted Mrs. Dobson. She set a platter of fried eggs and bacon on the table. "I am his daughter and he is my father and he'd better get used to it. And that police chief of yours had darn well better do something about those footprints, too. That has to be a crime."

"Arson, I imagine," said Bob.

"Call it whatever you like. It's got to stop. Now you boys eat. I'm going to town."

"You didn't have any breakfast," protested Tom.

"Who needs it?" snapped his mother. "Eat. Go ahead. And stay put, for Pete's sake. I'll be right back."

She snatched up her purse, which had been stowed on top of the refrigerator, rummaged for car keys, then strode down the hall and out the door. A second later, the boys heard the engine of the blue convertible.

"Mom kind of gets a second wind," said Tom, a little embarrassed.

"Good eggs," said Jupiter. He had served himself and was eating on his feet, leaning against the doorway. "I think we'd better do the dishes before she gets back."

"Your years with Aunt Mathilda have given you a sound sense of psychology," Bob said.

"Your mother is, of course, quite justified in being angry with your grandfather," Jupiter told young Tom. "However, I don't believe The Potter wanted to hurt her. He never wanted to hurt anybody. A lonely person, but very gentle, I think." Jupiter put down his plate in the sink and remembered again the men in the Cadillac and their confrontation with The Potter. He remembered The Potter standing in the driveway of the salvage yard, holding his medallion with his hand.

"The double-headed eagle," said Jupiter. "Tom, you said your grandfather sometimes sent you things which he had made. Did he ever send anything with a double-headed eagle?"

Tom thought a minute, then shook his head. "Mom likes birds," he told Jupiter. "He sent things with birds on them, mostly, but just regular birds— robins and bluebirds. No freaks like that plaque upstairs."

"But he wore the eagle on the medallion," said Jupiter, "and he used it when he designed that plaque—and a plaque for an empty room, incidentally. Now why would he go to the trouble to make a huge thing like that and install it in an empty room?"

Jupiter wiped his hands on a tea towel and started for the stairs. The other boys instantly abandoned their breakfasts and followed him up and into the room which had been occupied by Mrs. Dobson.

The crimson eagle glared at them from above the mantel.

Jupiter felt around the edges of the plaque. "It seems to be cemented into place," he said.

Tom Dobson ducked back into his own room and returned with a nail file. "Try this," he said.

Jupe pried at the edges of the ceramic piece. "No. It's up there to stay," he announced. "I think The Potter must have replastered the wall above the fireplace and put the plaque right into the plaster."

Jupe stepped back and looked up at the screaming bird. "What a job that must have been. It's a very large piece."

"Everybody's got to have a hobby," said Tom.

"Wait!" said Jupiter. "It isn't cast all in one piece. We need something to stand on."

Pete darted down to the kitchen and came back with one of the chairs. Jupiter stood on it and reached up toward the right head of the eagle. "That eye isn't the same as the other," he said. "It was cast separately." Jupiter pressed on the white porcelain of the eagle's eye. It gave under his fingers, and the boys heard a faint click. The entire wall above the mantel moved slightly.

"A secret door," said Jupiter. "Somehow, that makes sense." He stepped down from the chair, took hold of the ornate molding that edged the wall panel and tugged. The panel swung out on well-oiled hinges.

The boys crowded close to look into a compartment that was almost six inches deep. There were four shelves between the mantel and the ceiling, and they were piled with papers. Jupiter lifted one out.

"Why, they're only old copies of the Belleview *Register and Tribune*!" exclaimed Tom. He took the paper from Jupiter's hands and glanced through it. "This is the one that has the story about me," he said.

"How'd you make the news?" asked Bob.

"I won an essay contest," said Tom.

Jupiter had unfolded another paper—a much older one. "Your mother's wedding announcement," he said.

There were more—stories about the birth of young Tom, and about the death of his grandmother. There was a story on the grand opening of the Dobson Hardware Store, and one about a speech Tom's father had given on Veteran's Day. All the doings of the Dobsons had been chronicled in the papers, and The Potter had saved every one.

"A secret library," said Pete, "and you and your mother were the big secrets."

"Sure makes you feel appreciated," said young Tom.

"He was most reticent," said Jupiter. "No one even knew you existed. Odd. What is even more odd is the fact that there is nothing about The Potter himself in this secret library."

"Should there be?" said Pete. "He didn't like getting his name in the papers. Not that I could ever recall."

"True. And yet the men at Hilltop House yesterday mentioned that accounts of his artistry had appeared in periodicals. When accounts of your artistry appear in periodicals, the normal thing to do is to save the periodicals. Right?"

"Right," said Bob.

"So we can assume one of two things," said Jupiter. "Either The Potter does not have even the normal amount of vanity, or there were no accounts in periodicals—except for the photo spread in *Westways*. And The Potter did not even know of that until Saturday. He was not pleased when he did see it."

"Meaning?" asked Tom Dobson.

"Meaning that The Potter wanted to keep your existence a secret—and the last thing in the world he wanted for himself was acclaim. Perhaps he had very good reasons. Tom, we do not know why, but we learned last night that the two men who have rented Hilltop House are most interested in your grandfather. They appeared in Rocky Beach almost two months after the *Westways* spread came out with your grandfather's photograph. Does this suggest anything to you?"

"It suggests that Grandpa may have been on the lam," said Tom. "But from what?"

"Do you know anything about Lapathia?" asked Jupiter.

"Never heard of it. What is it?"

"It's a country—a small European country, where a political assassination took place many years ago."

Tom shrugged. "According to Grandma, my grandfather was from the Ukraine," he said.

"Have you ever heard the name Azimov?" asked Jupiter.

"Nope."

"That could not have been your grandfather's name before he changed it to Potter?"

"No. He had a very long name. Very long. You couldn't pronounce it."

Jupiter stood, pulling at his lip.

"He went to a lot of trouble to hide a bunch of old newspapers," said Tom. "He could have done it much easier, if it was all that important. He could have stuck them in a file with some old bills—you know, like 'The Purloined Letter' by Edgar Allan Poe."

Pete put a hand to the heavy plaque. "That would have made more sense," he said. "A thing like this in an empty room is bound to attract attention, if you're looking for attention."

"And he wasn't," said Jupiter. "It was the last thing in the world he wanted."

Jupiter bent to examine the fireplace beneath the mantel. It was spotless. Obviously no one had ever lighted a fire in it. Jupe went down on his knees and peered inside, looking up. "There is no chimney," he announced. "The fireplace is a sham."

"Probably The Potter built it himself," guessed Bob.

"In that case, why is this little trap here?" said Jupiter. He lifted a small metal flap which had been built into the floor of the fireplace. "When you have a real fireplace, you have one of these to sweep the ashes out. Why put one in a false fireplace, where there will never be ashes?"

Jupiter squeezed his hand into the opening in the brick floor of the fireplace. He touched paper. "There's something here!" he cried. "An envelope!" He edged it up and out, and let the little metal trap clank shut.

It was a brown Manila envelope sealed with a large blob of red wax.

"The other secret library behind the plaque was a decoy," Jupiter decided. He held up the envelope. "I think the real secret is here. Well, Tom, what do we do now? It belongs to your grandfather, and he is missing and you are our client. What do we do?"

"We open it," said Tom without hesitation.

"I was hoping you'd say that," murmured Bob.

Jupiter broke the seal on the envelope.

"Well?" said Tom.

Jupiter took out a single sheet of heavy parchment which had been folded three times. He unfolded it with great care.

"Well, what is it?" asked Tom.

Jupiter frowned. "I don't know. A certificate of some kind. It looks like a diploma or a degree, except that it's not big enough."

The boys crowded around Jupiter. "What kind of language is that?" asked Pete.

Bob shook his head. "Beats me," he said. "I never saw anything like it before."

Jupiter went to the window and held the hand-lettered document close to his eyes. "I can only recognize two things," he announced after a few moments. "One is the seal at the bottom. It is our old friend, the two-headed eagle. The other is a name —it's Kerenov. Someone at some time conferred some honor on one Alexis Kerenov. Have you ever heard that name, Tom?"

"No," said Tom. "It couldn't have been Grandfather. Like I said, his name was real, real long."

"You recall the name, Bob, don't you?" said Jupiter.

"You bet I do," said Bob. "Kerenov was the artisan who created the crown for old Federic Azimov."

Tom stared from one of them to the other. "Federic Azimov? Who's he?"

"He was the first king of Lapathia," Jupiter told him. "He lived 400 years ago."

Tom Dobson stared at the Investigators. "But what would that have to do with my grandfather?" he asked.

"We don't know," said Jupiter, "but we intend to find out."

13

The Odd Eagle

Jupiter Jones piled the copies of the Belleview newspaper neatly on the shelves in the compartment above the fireplace and swung the panel closed.

"Your mother will be back any minute," Jupiter said, "and I imagine Chief Reynolds will be with her. I have a strong feeling that we would be doing your grandfather a disservice if we turned the document we found over to the chief. The Three Investigators are following up certain lines of inquiry having to do with Lapathia and the royal family of the Azimovs. Do you agree, Tom, that we should be allowed to continue these until we have real evidence to present to the police?"

Tom scratched his head in bewilderment. "Wherever you are, you're way ahead of me," he said. "Okay. You keep the paper—for the time being. What about those newspapers behind the plaque?"

"It is possible that the police will discover the secret compartment," said Jupiter. "If so, there can be no harm done. I believe that is what the compartment was built for—to draw attention away from the real secret."

"I sure hope I get to meet my grandfather before all this is over," said Tom. "He must be a character."

"It will be an interesting experience," Jupiter promised him.

Bob looked out the window. "Here comes Mrs. Dobson now," he reported.

"Chief Reynolds with her?" asked Jupe.

"There's a squad car right behind her," said Bob.

"Omigosh! The dishes!" cried Pete.

"Indeed," said Jupiter Jones, and the boys dashed down the stairs. By the time Mrs. Dobson had parked and crossed the yard to the front door, Jupiter was running hot water into the sink, Tom was frantically scraping plates, and Bob stood by with a towel.

"Oh, how nice!" said Mrs. Dobson when she saw the activity in the kitchen.

"Delicious breakfast, Mrs. Dobson," said Pete.

Chief Reynolds, followed by Officer Haines, stalked into the kitchen after Mrs. Dobson. He ignored the other boys and focused his wrath on Jupiter. "Why didn't you call me last night?" he demanded.

"Mrs. Potter was upset," said Jupiter.

"And since when are you a member of the Ladies Aid Society?" demanded the chief. "Jupiter Jones, one of these days, you are going to get your fat head knocked clean off."

"Yes, sir," agreed Jupe.

"Flaming footprints!" snorted the chief. He

turned to Haines. "Search the house," he ordered.

"We did that, Chief," Jupiter reported. "There wasn't anyone here."

"You mind if we do it our way?" said the chief.

"No, sir."

"And get out, will you?" said the irate police chief. "Go on. Go and play stickball, or whatever it is normal kids do."

The boys fled to the yard.

"Is he always that grumpy?" Tom asked.

"Only when Jupe doesn't let him in on things," said Bob.

"That figures." Tom sat down on the steps between the two huge urns which were banded with double-headed eagles.

Jupiter frowned at one of the urns.

"What's your problem?" said Bob.

"One of these eagles has only one head," said Jupiter, puzzled.

The boys crowded around the urn. It was true. One of the birds in the bright band which decorated the piece was missing a head—the right-hand head. It looked like an ordinary, one-headed creature gazing off to the left.

"Interesting," said Jupiter.

Bob circled the other vase, examining the band of eagles. "All of these have two heads," he reported.

"Maybe my grandfather made a mistake," said Tom.

"The Potter does not make mistakes such as

this," said Jupiter. "His designs are always perfect. If he intended to put a band of double-headed eagles on this urn, he would have done so."

"It could be another decoy," said Bob, "like that secret compartment in the bedroom. Is there anything in it?"

Jupiter tried to lift the top off the urn. It did not budge. He tried to unscrew it, and it did not unscrew. He examined the sides of the piece, and the pedestal, which was cemented in place on the steps. He pressed on the single-headed eagle, as he had pressed on the eye embedded in the plaque. Nothing gave way.

"Really a decoy," he murmured. "It was never intended to be opened."

Chief Reynolds came out onto the porch. "If I didn't know better," he announced to anyone who cared to listen, "I'd say the place *was* haunted."

"It is mysterious," Jupiter agreed. He went on to tell the chief of the strange chemical odor he had detected on the newly burned footprints.

"Was it anything you recognized?" asked the chief. "Kerosene? Anything like that?"

"No," said Jupiter. "It was entirely unfamiliar— a sharp, acid smell."

"Hm," said the chief. "The lab has samples of the charred linoleum. Maybe they can find out something. You boys have anything else you can tell me about this thing?"

The Three Investigators looked at one another, and then at Tom Dobson. "No, sir," said Tom.

"Then you can leave," said the chief, rather curtly.

"Right," agreed Bob. "I have to go home and change my clothes and get to the library."

Jupiter made for his bicycle. "Aunt Mathilda will be wondering," he said.

The Three Investigators waved a hasty good-bye to Tom Dobson and started down the highway toward Rocky Beach. At the intersection near The Jones Salvage Yard, Jupiter pulled his bike to the curb. The other two boys also stopped.

"I wonder if the jolly fisherman is connected with the disturbances," said Jupiter.

"He's just a creep," declared Pete.

"Perhaps," said Jupiter. "However, he has a way of being around just before things happen—or just after. He was parked across from The Potter's when the house was searched and I was knocked down. He attempted to call on Mrs. Dobson last evening, not long before the second set of flaming footprints appeared. He could have been the man who shot at us from the hillside. We are sure the two men at Hilltop House didn't do that."

"But why would he?"

"Who knows?" said Jupe. "Perhaps he is a confederate of the men at Hilltop House. If we could solve the secret of The Potter, we might know many things." Jupe reached into his pocket and took out the document he had discovered in the dummy fireplace. "Here." He handed it to Bob. "Is there any possibility that you could identify the language on this parchment, or perhaps even translate it?"

"I'm willing to bet it's in Lapathian," said Bob. "I'll do what I can."

"Good. And also, if we could find out more about the Azimovs it could be helpful. The name Kerenov on that document is most provocative."

"The crown-maker? Right. I'll try." Bob pocketed the envelope and rode on.

"What time is it?" Pete asked nervously. "My mom will be having a fit."

"It's only nine," said Jupiter. "Will she be so worried? I thought we might pay a visit to Miss Hopper."

"At the Seabreeze Inn? What's she got to do with it?"

"Not a thing. She is, however, the landlady of that jolly fisherman, and she usually takes an acute interest in the welfare of her guests."

"Okay," said Pete. "Let's see her. But let's not be all day about it. I want to get home before Mom starts phoning your Aunt Mathilda."

"That would be wise," Jupiter conceded.

The boys found Miss Hopper in the lobby of the Seabreeze Inn, in worried consultation with Marie, the maid.

"It can't be helped," Miss Hopper was saying. "You'll just have to skip 113 and come back to it after lunch."

"Serve him right if I skipped it altogether," snapped Marie, and she banged out of the lobby pushing her cart with cleaning utensils in front of her.

"Something wrong, Miss Hopper?" asked Jupiter.

"Oh, Jupiter. And Pete. Good morning. It's nothing important, really. It's only that Mr. Farrier has a 'Do Not Disturb' sign on his door and Marie can't get in to do his room. It always upsets her when she can't follow her regular routine."

Miss Hopper hesitated for a moment, then said with a touch of slyness, "I heard Mr. Farrier come in last night. Well, actually it was this morning. Three o'clock."

"That's interesting," said Jupiter. "Most fishermen are early morning people."

"I have always understood that," said Miss Hopper. "Mr. Farrier was so attentive to young Mrs. Dobson yesterday, I wondered if he might not be helping her get settled."

"Until three in the morning?" exclaimed Pete.

"No, Miss Hopper," said Jupiter. "We have just come from The Potter's, and Mr. Farrier did not spend the evening with Mrs. Dobson."

"Now where do you suppose the man could have been until that hour?" wondered Miss Hopper. "Well, it is his own concern, I am sure. And how is poor, dear Mrs. Dobson this morning? I saw her drive by earlier."

"She is reasonably well, under the circumstances. She came into town to file an official report with Chief Reynolds. She wants her father found." Jupiter had no hesitation about confiding this much to

Miss Hopper, who always found things out anyway.

"Most proper," said Miss Hopper. "What a strange thing for The Potter to do—going off that way without a word to anyone. But then, he has always been a strange man."

"That's for sure," said Pete.

"Well, we must be going, Miss Hopper," said Jupiter. "We only thought you would like to know that Mrs. Dobson and her son are settled in at The Potter's house. You always take such an interest in your guests."

"How nice of you, Jupiter," said Miss Hopper.

"And I hope Mr. Farrier wakes up before lunch."

"It would make Marie happy," said Miss Hopper. "Poor man. One shouldn't be too hard on him. He has such dreadful luck!"

"Oh?" prompted Jupiter.

"Yes. He's been here four days just for the fishing, and he hasn't caught a thing."

"Terribly frustrating," said Jupiter, and he and Pete took their leave of Miss Hopper.

"Now where do you go at three in the morning in Rocky Beach?" asked Pete, once they were outside.

"Several places occur to me," said Jupiter. "One could, of course, try fishing by moonlight. Or perhaps one could be waiting on a hillside with a gun. Or one might amuse oneself by frightening people with flaming footprints."

"I might buy that last," said Pete, "if there was

any way he could have gotten into that house. Jupe, all the downstairs windows are locked, and most of them are painted shut. There are two locks and a bolt on the front door and one regular lock and a dead-bolt lock on the back. He couldn't have gotten in."

"Someone did," Jupiter pointed out.

"For my money, only one person could," said Pete. "The Potter would be the only one with the keys."

"Which brings us back to the question of why?" Jupe reminded him.

"Maybe he doesn't like house guests," said Pete.

"You know that's ridiculous," said Jupiter.

"The alternative is even sillier," said Pete. "He's gone off and kicked the bucket someplace, and then come back to haunt the house." And with that, Pete mounted his bicycle and pedaled away toward his home.

Jupiter returned to The Jones Salvage Yard to confront an anxious Aunt Mathilda and a concerned Uncle Titus.

"How is Mrs. Dobson?" was Aunt Mathilda's first question.

"She's better this morning," Jupiter reported. "Last night she was extremely emotional—not to say hysterical."

"Why?" asked Uncle Titus.

"There was a second set of those flaming footprints," said Jupiter. "On the stairs, this time."

"Merciful gracious to heavens!" cried Aunt Mathilda. "And she still insisted on staying in that house?"

"Aunt Mathilda, I do not believe she was in any condition to move last night," said Jupiter.

"Jupiter, you should have told me," scolded Aunt Mathilda. She turned to her husband. "Titus Andronicus Jones!"

Uncle Titus always paid strict attention when he was addressed by all three of his names. "Yes, Mathilda," he said.

"Get the truck," said Aunt Mathilda. "We must go up there and persuade that poor, misguided child to get out of that terrible house before something happens to her."

Uncle Titus started for the truck.

"As for you, Jupiter," said Aunt Mathilda severely, "I am very much annoyed with you. You take too much upon yourself. What you need is some work to do to keep you out of mischief."

Jupiter didn't answer this. Aunt Mathilda was an ardent advocate of work even when there was no mischief afoot.

"There are those marble garden ornaments your uncle brought from that wrecked house in Beverly Hills," said Aunt Mathilda. "They are absolutely filthy. You know where the bucket is, and the soap."

"Yes, Aunt Mathilda," said Jupiter.

"And plenty of elbow grease!" ordered his aunt.

Aunt Mathilda and Uncle Titus clattered away in the truck. Jupiter cleared a space in the back of the salvage yard and set to work with hot sudsy water on the marble figures and the garden urns. The things were coated with years of soil and grit and mold. Jupiter scrubbed away, cleaning the face of a chubby cherub who held up an apple. Hans found him there.

"I see your aunt been talking to you," said Hans, eyeing the scrub brush and the bucket.

Jupiter nodded, wiped off the marble cherub, and turned to a bulging urn with grapes clustered on its sides.

"Where is everybody?" Hans wanted to know. "I been over to house, and nobody there. Nobody in office, either."

"Aunt Mathilda and Uncle Titus have gone up to The Potter's house to see Mrs. Dobson," reported Jupiter.

"Huh!" snorted Hans. "I don't go to that place— not for a million dollars. That place is haunted. That crazy Potter, he's walking around up there in his bare feet. You saw it. I saw it."

Jupiter sat back on his heels. "We saw the footprints," he reminded Hans. "We did not see The Potter."

"Who else could it be?" demanded Hans.

Jupiter didn't answer. He stared at the urn, which was an ungainly piece, and he thought of The Potter, who made such handsome things. "The urns on The Potter's porch are much better than this one," said Jupiter.

"Yah! Yah! His stuff's good. But he was crazy anyway."

"No, I don't think so," said Jupiter. "But I wonder why one of the eagles on that urn has only one head."

"Nothing wrong with one head on eagle," declared Hans.

"True. Except that The Potter seemed to prefer them with two," answered Jupiter Jones.

14

The Jolly Fisherman

It was noon before Aunt Mathilda and Uncle Titus returned to the salvage yard with the information that Eloise Dobson was the most stubborn creature on the face of the earth. In spite of Chief Reynolds' urging and Aunt Mathilda's considerable powers of persuasion, Mrs. Dobson had firmly, and rather angrily, announced that no one was going to drive her out of her father's house.

"She was ready enough to go last night," said Jupiter.

"Then you should have seen that she left," snapped Aunt Mathilda, and she stormed across the street to the house to make lunch.

Jupiter rinsed the last of the marble pieces with the hose and went in to take a shower. After lunch, he returned to the salvage yard. His aunt had neglected to issue any instructions for the afternoon, so Jupiter made his way to Headquarters through Tunnel Two, and then escaped unseen from the salvage yard by exiting through Red Gate Rover. He then hurried down to the Rocky Beach Police Department.

Jupiter found Chief Reynolds brooding behind his desk.

"Any little thing on your mind, Jones?" asked the chief.

"There is a man staying at the Seabreeze Inn who has been rather overattentive to Mrs. Dobson," said Jupiter.

"In that department," said the chief, "I think Mrs. Dobson can take care of herself."

"That is not what concerns me," said Jupiter. "He has led Miss Hopper to believe that he is here to fish. However, he does not catch anything."

"So? He's got bum luck."

"That is certainly possible, but his car was parked across from The Potter's house on Saturday when I was attacked in The Potter's office. Also, he attempted to visit Mrs. Dobson last evening not long before that second set of flaming footprints appeared in the house. And then, there are his clothes."

"What about his clothes?"

"They are all brand new, so far as I can judge," said Jupiter. "It is almost as if he were costumed for a part in a film. The clothes, incidentally, do not match the car he drives. That is old and somewhat battered. It is a tan Ford. Perhaps you might wish to wire to Sacramento to see how the car is registered. The man calls himself Farrier."

"He may just do that because it's his name," said the chief. "Look, Jones, I know you think you're the greatest thing since Sherlock Holmes, but I wish you'd knock off this business of snooping around where you're not wanted. And I've got real problems. That Mrs. Dobson seems to expect me to produce her missing father—if he *is* her father—by nightfall, if not sooner. With my overwhelming staff of eight men, I am to go out and scour the Pacific Coast Range and find a man who doesn't want to be found. I am also expected to figure out how somebody got into a locked house and set the stairs on fire."

"Have you had any report from the lab on the charred linoleum?" asked Jupiter.

"When I do, you may be the last to know," said Chief Reynolds. "Now go away and let me have my headache in peace."

"You don't plan to wire Sacramento?" Jupiter persisted.

"No, I don't. And if you go bothering that Farrier guy, I will personally have you declared a public nuisance."

"Very well," said Jupiter. He left the chief's office and proceeded with all due speed to the Seabreeze Inn. He noted with satisfaction that the tan Ford was not in the parking area. Miss Hopper, he knew, was addicted to afternoon naps and might well be dozing peacefully in her own apartment. With the exception of a stray guest or two, that left only Marie the maid to be reckoned with.

The lobby of the Seabreeze Inn was deserted, and the door behind the desk was closed. Jupiter tiptoed around the desk. Miss Hopper was an extremely meticulous innkeeper, and Jupiter knew her very well. He found the spare key to room 113 where he knew it would be—in its properly numbered slot in the bottom drawer of Miss Hopper's desk. Jupiter extracted the key without making a sound, put the key in his pocket, and strolled out onto the verandah. Marie was nowhere to be seen, and there were no guests lounging on the terrace which overlooked the beach.

Jupiter put his hands in his pockets and sauntered along the verandah. When he reached the door of room 113, he stopped and waited, listening. No one stirred anywhere in the inn.

"Mr. Farrier?" he called, knocking softly. Mr. Farrier did not answer.

With great care, Jupiter slid the key into the lock, opened the door, and stepped into the room.

"Mr. Farrier?" he said again softly.

But the room was empty—empty and tidy. Marie had had time to make up the bed and vacuum the carpet.

Jupiter eased the door shut and set to work. The bureau drawers were empty, and so were the desk drawers. Mr. Farrier had not troubled to unpack his handsome suitcases—except for several crisp and sporty jackets which hung in the closet along with half a dozen spotless turtleneck shirts and several pairs of cleanly creased blue duck slacks. Jupiter felt the pockets of these garments, but they were empty.

Next, Jupe turned his attention to the suitcases. There were two. One stood open on a little bench at the foot of the bed. It contained about what one would expect a suitcase to contain—pajamas, socks, a pair of sneakers which looked as if they had never been worn, underwear, and, wadded at the bottom of the bag, a few pieces of clothing in need of laundering.

The second suitcase stood on the floor next to the bench. It was closed, but when Jupe tried it he discovered that it was not locked. There were more clothes—all new, and bearing the labels of various Los Angeles men's shops. One shirt still had the price tag attached, and Jupiter almost gasped when he saw how much the thing had cost.

Jupiter's probing fingers touched paper in the bottom of the suitcase. He lifted the clothes out, careful not to disarrange anything, and stared at a piece of folded newspaper. It was the classified section of the *Los Angeles Times*. An item in the "Personals" section was circled. It read: "Nicholas. I am waiting. Write Alexis at P.O. Box 213, Rocky Beach, Ca."

Jupiter lifted the paper out. There was another sheet of newsprint beneath it. This was part of the classified section of the *New York Daily News,* and an identical advertisement appeared there. There was also a copy of the *Chicago Tribune,* with the same notice. Jupiter glanced at the dates on the newspapers. They were all the April 21 editions of that year.

Jupiter frowned, put the *Chicago Tribune* back where he had found it, placed the *Daily News* back on top of that, and the Los Angeles newspaper on top of that. He then replaced the clothing in the suitcase, closed the case, and put it down again on the floor.

Whatever the jaunty fisherman had come for, Ju-

piter Jones decided, it had little or nothing to do
with fish.

Jupiter quickly inspected the bathroom—which
contained only shaving gear and clean towels—and
was on his way to the door when he heard brisk
footsteps on the verandah outside. A key rattled in
the lock of room 113.

Jupe looked around wildly, decided that he
would not be able to squeeze himself under the
bed, and dodged into the closet. He took shelter
behind one of Mr. Farrier's clean jackets and held
his breath.

Jupe heard Farrier come into the room. The man
was humming a tuneless hum. He crossed to the
bed, stopped there for a moment or two, and then
went on into the bathroom. The bathroom door
closed and Jupiter heard water running in the
basin.

Jupiter slipped out of the closet and sped on his
toes toward the door. He had it open in a second.
The water continued noisily running in the bathroom. Jupiter backed out onto the verandah, pulling the door closed as he went. The instant before
it shut completely, he saw that Mr. Farrier had
dropped something on the bed.

The supposedly jolly fisherman had a gun!

15

Jupe Has a Plan

Pete had finished mowing the lawn and was mixing a lemonade when the telephone rang.

"Pete?" said Jupiter Jones. "Can you come to Headquarters right after supper?"

"I can if it isn't going to be another all-night thing," said Pete. "Mom's not going to go for that twice in a row."

"It won't be an all-night thing," promised Jupiter. "I have some new and interesting information which may help our client. I have left a message for Bob. Perhaps, when he returns from the library, he will also have helpful information for us."

"That we can use," said Pete.

Jupiter's hopes were well-founded. When Bob appeared at Headquarters that evening, he was almost staggering under the weight of two large books which had pieces of paper tucked in to mark various pages.

"A Lapathian dictionary," said Bob brightly. "Lapathian-English, that is. You wouldn't believe how hard they are to come by. We had to arrange a special loan from the big library in Los Angeles. My father picked the books up on his way home from work. The second one is a complete history of Lapathia."

"Great!" exclaimed Pete.

"Have you been able to decipher the document we found at The Potter's?" asked Jupe.

"Most of it. The rest we can guess," said Bob. "Thank heavens Lapathian isn't like Russian. They use a regular alphabet. If I had to translate from some other kind of writing, I think I'd just go shoot myself."

"What is the document?" Jupiter asked.

Bob took the folded parchment from between the pages of the dictionary and put it down on the desk. Next to it he put a piece of paper on which he had worked out, in pencil and with many erasures and crossings out, the message of the parchment.

"It goes kind of like this," said Bob. " 'Know all men that on this day, the 25th of August of the year 1920, Alexis Kerenov, having attained his majority and having sworn fealty to his monarch, is named Duke of Malenbad and to his care and conscience are entrusted the crown and scepter of Lapathia, he to guard them with his body against all enemies for the peace of the monarch.' "

Bob looked up. "That's about it," he said. "There's the seal with the eagle, and there's a signature, but you can't read it. People are sloppy about signatures."

"And the more important they are," said Jupiter, "the sloppier they tend to get. Could it be Azimov?"

Bob shrugged. "It could be anything," he said. "It probably is Azimov, or some variation, because the Kerenov family turned out to be big wheels in Lapathia. Boris Kerenov didn't just fade away and disappear. He hung around and was ever so helpful." Bob opened the second book he had brought to a place which he had previously marked with paper. "This book's indexed," he said happily, "so we don't have to wade all the way through. Boris Kerenov, who made the crown for old Duke Federic, then advised Federic when Federic decided to be king. He helped Federic lay out the streets around the castle at Madanhoff, and he superintended things when the castle itself was enlarged. He figured that kings need scepters, so he designed and made the scepter of the Azimovs. Federic was duly grateful and named him Duke of Malenbad. Malenbad, by one of those interesting coincidences, happened to be the duchy which had formerly been ruled by Ivan the Bold."

"Wait a second," interrupted Pete. "Let's keep track of the cast here. Ivan the Bold. Wasn't he the guy who stood up to Duke Federic and wouldn't swear the oath of loyalty? And he got very dead as a result."

"And his head was stuck up on the castle at Madanhoff. He's the one. Kerenov got Ivan's ruby for the imperial crown, and he got Ivan's estates for his very own, and he got himself named a duke and also keeper of the royal jewels—which makes sense since he made them—and he got very, very rich and the Kerenovs stayed that way from that day on. This book is full of Kerenovs. All the first sons of the first sons became Dukes of Malenbad, and also keepers of the crown and scepter."

Bob turned to another part of the book. "The Kerenovs are almost more interesting than the Azimovs," he said. "They lived for a while in old Ivan's castle at Malenbad, but along about 300 years ago they abandoned the castle and moved to the capital at Madanhoff, and you're going to love the reason why."

"Why are we going to love it?" asked Jupiter.

"It's so pat, I can't believe it," said Bob. "It seems there was a bit of trouble at Malenbad. One of the Kerenov daughters—her name was Olga— was accused of practicing witchcraft."

"Wasn't that tricky?" asked Pete. "I mean, wouldn't it be kind of dangerous to accuse the duke's daughter of being a witch?"

"Not as tricky as you might think," said Bob. "It was one of those hysteria things, much like the epidemic of supposed witchcraft at Salem, and everybody was accusing everybody. The girl had had the bad fortune to fall out with her father because she wanted to marry the local innkeeper, and he did not approve. Besides, he was accused himself. He was worried about his own skin, and he had to call on the then-ruling Azimov to come to his defense. So the girl was burned at the stake."

"Oh, wow!" said Pete.

"Burned?" Jupiter came to rigid attention. "And then the Kerenovs left their castle at Malenbad?"

"Yes. You see, after she was burned, the girl—or

I guess you could say her ghost—kept coming back to the castle and tramping around and leaving . . ."

"Flaming footprints!" cried Jupiter.

"Right!" said Bob. "So the castle was deserted, and is now a ruin, and the Kerenovs stayed on in the capital until that revolution we know about in 1925, when they disappeared. There isn't another mention of them in the entire book."

The Three Investigators sat in silence for a moment, digesting this information.

"I will hazard a guess—a very well-informed guess, thanks to Bob—at what Mr. Alexander Potter's real name is," said Jupiter at last.

"If you guess that it's Alexis Kerenov, I'm with you," said Bob.

"But Tom said it was a long name," protested Pete. "It had lots of c's and z's in it."

"No doubt he was not using his real name when he met Tom's grandmother," surmised Jupiter. "And remember her description of him?"

"He smelled like wet clay?" said Pete.

"Yes. And he was extremely nervous and had three locks on every door. To this day he is a great believer in locks. The Potter is a man with a secret, and he is also a man trying to send a message."

"What?" asked Bob.

Jupiter quickly recounted his adventure of the afternoon. He told of the search of the jolly fisherman's room, and of the gun, and also of the newspapers with identical advertisements in the classified columns. "A New York paper, a *Los Angeles*

Times and the *Chicago Tribune*," he said. "All published on the same date—April 21. All begging Nicholas to write to Alexis at a post office box in Rocky Beach."

"Nicholas?" echoed Bob.

"Your index got a Nicholas we can use?" asked Pete.

"Nicholas was the name of the oldest son of William IV of Lapathia," said Bob. He turned several more pages in his book and shoved the volume around so that the other two boys could see the last photograph ever taken of the royal family of Lapathia. There was His Majesty, William IV, his extravagant wife, and four sons, ranging from a tall young man who stood directly behind His Majesty to a boy who was about ten. "The one right behind the king is Grand Duke Nicholas," said Bob.

"And William IV was the one who fell off the balcony," said Jupiter. "According to the account in the encyclopedia, the queen took poison. What happened to Nicholas?"

"He is said to have hanged himself."

"And the other children?"

"The two middle boys also hanged themselves, according to the generals who engineered the takeover. The little one accidentally fell in his bath and was drowned."

"Hm!" Jupe pulled at his lip. "Let us suppose, just for the sake of argument, that the Grand Duke Nicholas did not hang himself. How old would he be today?"

"Over seventy," said Bob.

"How old would you think The Potter is?"

"Well, somewhere around there. Jupe, you don't think The Potter could really be the Grand Duke?"

"No, I do not. I think he is Alexis Kerenov, who vanished on the day the Azimov family was destroyed. What day was that, by the way?"

Bob consulted his book. "April 21, 1925."

"And on April 21 of this year, someone named Alexis, who we suspect is The Potter, inserted an advertisement in newspapers in widely separate parts of the country imploring someone named Nicholas to communicate with him. The advertisement would seem to have drawn Mr. Farrier, who is really no fisherman at all, to Rocky Beach. He could not possibly be Nicholas Azimov. He is too young."

"Perhaps the same advertisement got those two ginks from Lapathia here," said Bob. "By the way, there's a bit on General Kaluk. He was in at the kill, and he has been one of the ruling generals of Lapathia ever since. There's a picture of him on page 433."

Jupe turned the leaves to page 433. "The caption indicates that the general was 23 when this was taken in 1926," he said. "He hasn't changed a great deal. He didn't have any hair then, either. I wonder if he's naturally bald or if he shaves his head. That would be a novel way to prevent the appearance of aging. You shave your head and your eyebrows, and nothing will ever go gray."

"Should work fine, if you don't sag too much," declared Pete.

"He most certainly has not sagged," said Jupiter. "He would be about the same age as the Grand Duke Nicholas—if the Grand Duke Nicholas is still alive—and as The Potter. I don't think, however, that it was the advertisement which brought him to Rocky Beach. I think it was that photo spread in *Westways*. Demetrieff is evidently a resident of Los Angeles, since the Lapathian Board of Trade maintains an office there. Remember, Kaluk said that The Potter had been written up in our periodicals. So far as I know, *Westways* is the only periodical which has ever published a photograph of The Potter. Demetrieff could have seen it, and the eagle medallion, and informed his superiors in Lapathia."

"And in comes the general."

"Yes. A thoroughly distasteful person. However, all this speculation does not bring us any closer to helping our client, Tom Dobson. It seems clear that someone who knows the family history of the Kerenovs, and the tale of the flaming footprints in the haunted castle, is trying to frighten Mrs. Dobson and Tom out of the house. There can be only one reason for this. They believe that there is something of value in the house. Now, Mrs. Dobson knows nothing of the Kerenovs and she has a remarkable stubborn streak, so she refuses to move. If we can persuade Mrs. Dobson and Tom to leave the place and return to the Seabreeze Inn—or perhaps even go into Los Angeles—we may see some action more significant than flaming footprints."

"Like baiting a trap," said Pete.

"Yes, except that in this case, the trap must be empty. Mrs. Dobson and Tom cannot be in the house. The two men at Hilltop House have not made a move since she arrived, and the man who calls himself Farrier has done nothing more effective than to attempt to have coffee with Mrs. Dobson. And of course The Potter remains among the missing."

"So we get Mrs. Dobson to move out, and then we watch," said Pete.

"That's right. We will have to be very careful."

"You will have to be very persuasive," said Pete. "There are times when Mrs. Dobson reminds me of your Aunt Mathilda."

16

The Trap is Sprung

It was well after seven when The Three Investigators reached The Potter's house. Pete pounded on the front door and Jupiter called out to identify himself.

Young Tom Dobson opened the door. "Your timing is perfect," he said. "Come on in."

The Investigators trailed after Tom to the kitchen, where Mrs. Dobson sat in one of the straight chairs and watched a pair of green flames flicker and die out on the linoleum near the cellar door.

"You know," she said, without much emotion, "this sort of thing loses its shock value after a while."

"Where were you when it happened?" asked Jupiter.

"Upstairs," said Mrs. Dobson. "Something went 'bang' and Tom came down to see what, and there were some more of these nice, cheering footprints."

"Want to search the house?" Tom Dobson invited. "I was about to do that when you guys showed up."

"I doubt that we would learn anything new," said Jupe.

"We've already searched it," put in Pete. "And so have Chief Reynolds' men."

"Have you had any news from the chief, incidentally?" Jupiter asked.

"Not a word," said Eloise Dobson.

"Mrs. Dobson," said Jupe, getting quickly to the main purpose of his visit, "we think you should leave here—and the sooner the better."

"I will not!" said Mrs. Dobson. "I came to see my father, and I am going no place until I do see him."

"The Seabreeze Inn isn't far," suggested Bob gently.

"Aunt Mathilda would be glad to put you up for a night or two," offered Jupiter.

"You wouldn't have to leave Rocky Beach," urged Pete. "Just leave this house."

Mrs. Dobson glared at the three of them. "What's up with you three?" she demanded.

"Hasn't it occurred to you that someone is trying to frighten you out of here?" said Jupiter.

"Of course it has occurred to me. I would have to be the world's champion dimwit for it not to occur to me. Well, I don't scare that easy."

"We believe that the person who is creating the flaming footprints is not simply a trickster," said Jupiter. "Whoever he is, he knows a great deal about your father, and about your father's family history. He knows more than you do—although he cannot suspect how little you really have been told. It is our theory that he wants a clear field. He wants to search this house without interruption. We suggest that you give him the opportunity. Move out now, while it is still light. Give him a chance to see that you are going. Then drive down to Rocky Beach and remain there. Pete, Bob, and I will watch to see what takes place after you leave."

"You can't mean that!" cried Mrs. Dobson.

"We do," said Jupiter.

"You want me to clear out and let this oddball who's been running around making flaming footprints come romping through my father's house?"

"I think that is the only way we will ever discover the purpose behind all of this—your father's disappearance, the search of the house which occurred the day you arrived, the flaming footprints —everything."

Eloise Dobson frowned up at Jupiter. "Chief Reynolds told me about you," she said. "And you, too, Bob. And Pete. He said, if I remember correctly, that your talent for stirring up trouble is only exceeded by your knack for figuring things out."

"A mixed compliment," said Jupiter.

"All right." Mrs. Dobson stood up. "Tom and I pack and move out, with all the fuss possible. Then you boys hide someplace and watch the house. I'll go along with you partway. We'll even leave the door open so that the nut—whoever he is—can get in. Although he doesn't seem to have had any trouble doing that so far, and whenever he wants to. But unless the guy is really hung up on ceramics, I don't see what he expects to find. This place is full of nothing."

"Perhaps it is not," said Jupiter. "We will see."

"One thing," said Mrs. Dobson. "I would like to know what this big, dark secret is that is hidden on my father's family tree."

"Mrs. Dobson, we really do not have time to explain," said Jupiter. "It will be dark in half an hour. Please, let's hurry and get you moved out!"

"Okay. But there's another thing."

"Yes?" asked Jupiter.

"The minute Tom and I get into town, I'm going straight to that police chief and tell him what you're doing," announced Mrs. Dobson. "If somebody starts to play rough, you're going to need help."

The Three Investigators paused. Then, "That might be a wise idea," said Jupiter.

"Hey, Jupe, it will wreck everything if a police car comes roaring up here!" protested Pete.

"I am sure Mrs. Dobson will be able to persuade Chief Reynolds not to come roaring," said Jupiter. "We will ride partway back to Rocky Beach on our bikes," he told Mrs. Dobson. "When we are out of sight of the house, we will stop, conceal the bicycles in the underbrush beside the road, and return here. The scrub growth on the hillside is especially thick right now. No one on the road will see us, and we will not be seen from Hilltop House, either. Tell Chief Reynolds that we will be keeping watch from just beyond the oleander hedge behind the house."

"Say, can we move now?" pleaded Bob. There was a note of urgency in his voice. "It's getting dark!"

"Come on, Tom," said Mrs. Dobson.

The two went up the stairs, two steps at a time, and The Three Investigators, waiting in the kitchen, heard drawers open and close and closet doors bang and suitcases thump onto the floors.

In four minutes Eloise Dobson came swiftly down the stairs carrying a square cosmetic case and a small suitcase. Tom followed her with two larger bags.

"A record!" Jupiter applauded. "Did you bring everything—toothbrushes—everything?"

"Everything," said Mrs. Dobson. "But it's going to be a mess when I unpack."

"That can always be straightened out later," said Jupiter. He took the small suitcase from Mrs. Dobson, and Pete relieved Tom of one of the bigger bags. Jupe looked around. "Let's go," he said.

They started down the hall toward the front door. As they passed the office, Mrs. Dobson suddenly balked. "Wait!" she cried. "Tom, get the box!"

"What box?" asked Pete.

"I went through my father's things," said Mrs. Dobson. Her tone was a bit defiant. "I wasn't snooping. I just was wondering—you know—and I found a box with some personal things in it. Nothing important. A picture of my mother and father taken on their wedding day, and a bunch of letters from my mother and some from me, and—Jupiter, I don't want anybody pawing through that stuff."

"I understand, Mrs. Dobson," said Jupiter. He took the second suitcase from Tom Dobson, and

Tom ducked into The Potter's office and emerged with a cardboard carton about a foot square. "My grandfather seems to have saved everything," he said.

Pete got the front door open, and the procession filed out past the two urns toward Mrs. Dobson's car, which stood near The Potter's supply shack.

Jupiter raised his voice. "I'm sorry you've decided to leave, Mrs. Dobson," he said.

"Huh?" said Eloise Dobson.

"Act frightened," whispered Jupiter.

"Oh!" said Mrs. Dobson. Then she raised her voice. She became almost shrill. "Jupiter Jones, if you think I'm going to hang around here while somebody burns the house down around my ears, you're crazy."

She put her cosmetic case down on the ground beside the car and opened the trunk.

"So far as I'm concerned," she announced, for all the world to hear, "I wish I'd never had a father. I wish I'd been born an orphan."

Mrs. Dobson energetically hurled suitcases into the trunk of the car. "And if I never see Rocky Beach—or this house—again, it will be soon enough for me! Tom, give me that box!"

Tom handed the box of old letters to his mother, and she started to cram it into the car. Suddenly, "Hold it!" said a voice from beside the Potter's shack.

The Three Investigators and the Dobsons turned. There, in the dense, golden light of the sunset, stood the jaunty fisherman, holding a gun.

"Everybody just stand quietly," said Farrier. "Don't move and you won't get hurt." The fisherman trained his gun on Eloise Dobson.

"I think," said Pete, "that something went wrong with our schedule."

"Give me the box," ordered Farrier. "Better still, open the box and dump it out on the ground."

"It's only some old letters to my grandfather," said Tom Dobson.

"Open it!" snapped Farrier. "I want to see."

"Don't argue with the man," advised Jupiter.

Tom sighed, hauled the square carton out of the trunk, opened and upended it. A mass of envelopes slid out into a heap on the ground.

"It *was* filled with letters!" exclaimed the jaunty fisherman. He sounded genuinely surprised.

"You were expecting a diamond tiara or something?" asked Tom Dobson.

The man called Farrier took one step forward. "What do you—?" he began. Then he checked himself. "The suitcases," he ordered. "Take them back into the house. I think they're too small, but we'll see."

Eloise Dobson knelt and scooped the letters into the cardboard carton, while the boys removed the suitcases from the trunk of the blue convertible. Then the Dobsons and The Three Investigators marched back into The Potter's house, with Mr. Farrier and his gun bringing up the rear.

In the hallway, Eloise Dobson fumed as the boys were forced to empty her suitcases out onto the floor. Young Tom's bag was also opened, and its

contents spread out for the inspection of the inso-
lent Mr. Farrier.

"So you didn't find it," said Farrier at last. "I
was sure, when I saw that cardboard box. . . ."

"Find what, for heaven's sake?" demanded Mrs.
Dobson.

"You don't know?" said Farrier. His voice was
very smooth. "No, you really don't know. Just as
well. In fact, my dear, charming Mrs. Dobson, it's
just as well if you never find out. Now, everybody
down in the cellar!"

"I will not!" cried Eloise Dobson.

"Yes, Mrs. Dobson, you will," said Farrier. "I
have already searched the cellar. The walls are
solid brick, the floors are cement, undisturbed for
decades. It will make an excellent resting place for
you while I finish my business. You see, there are
no windows in that cellar."

"It was *you* who searched the house on Saturday," accused Jupiter.

"Unfortunately, I did not have time to finish,"
said Farrier. "I found only one treasure on that oc-
casion." Farrier took a huge bunch of keys from his
pocket.

"The Potter's keys," said Jupiter.

"The second set, I assume," smirked Farrier. "It
was thoughtful of him to leave them in his desk. All
right, everybody. Move!"

The Dobsons and the Investigators moved, down
the hall and through the kitchen and then into the
cellar. Mrs. Dobson stopped only long enough to
click the light switch at the top of the stairs before

she went down into the bare, brick-walled place.

"You shouldn't be too uncomfortable here," said Farrier from the top of the stairs. "And no doubt someone will miss you before long and come looking for you."

With that, the jaunty fisherman closed the cellar door on them. A key turned in the lock, then was removed. The bolt on the door slid into place.

"I wish my grandfather hadn't been such a fanatic about locks," mourned young Tom.

"Oh, I don't know," said Jupiter Jones. He sat down on the cellar stairs and looked around. "It is not the ideal place in which to spend protracted periods of time, but it is far more comfortable than being tied up. I am sure that our guess was correct, and that the man who calls himself Farrier will now search the house thoroughly. It must have been that carton full of letters that did it. When he saw that, he decided that we had found what he is looking for. Our trap has been sprung."

"Yes, it has," said Pete bitterly, "only we're the ones who got caught."

17

The Other Watchers

The Dobsons and The Three Investigators arranged themselves as comfortably as possible on the cellar stairs and listened as, above them, the bogus fisherman searched The Potter's house.

Drawers in the kitchen were pulled open. Cupboard doors banged. Footsteps hurried into the pantry and cans tumbled to the floor. Walls were knocked.

They heard Farrier retreat from the kitchen and go down the hall to The Potter's office. There was a heavy, wrenching sound, and a thud that shook dust down around their ears. "He's knocked over the file," Pete decided.

The Potter's ancient desk was moved, screeching a protest against the bare boards of the floors. Then again there came the sounds of walls being thumped.

"Did the police find The Potter's secret library?" Jupiter asked Tom.

"No, they didn't," Tom reported.

"You boys have been holding out on me," declared Eloise Dobson. "What secret library?"

"It's nothing, Mom," said Tom. "Just a bunch of

old newspapers behind that eagle plaque in your room."

"Now why would anyone hide a bunch of old newspapers?" asked Mrs. Dobson.

"To give a searcher something to find," said Jupiter.

There was a crash from overhead.

"Oh, dear!" said Mrs. Dobson. "That must be the big vase in the hall."

"A pity," said Jupiter.

Farrier's footsteps crossed the hall and sounded heavily on the stairs.

"He must be the one who planted all those flaming footprints!" decided Mrs. Dobson suddenly.

"Undoubtedly," said Jupiter. "He had the keys, and could come and go as he pleased. He would have used the back door, I am sure, since the front door had a slide bolt."

"And the footsteps . . ." began Tom.

Jupiter held up his hand suddenly. "Listen."

They were silent. After a moment, "I don't hear anything," whispered Tom Dobson.

"Someone came up onto the back porch," said Jupiter. "They tried the door and then went down again."

"Oh, good!" said Eloise Dobson. "Let's yell!"

"Please don't, Mrs. Dobson," said Bob earnestly. "You see, there isn't only this Farrier creep. There's these two real sinister types up at Hilltop House."

"The Peeping Toms?" said Mrs. Dobson.

"I am afraid they are more sinister than that," Jupiter informed her. "They rented Hilltop House for a definite reason—because it overlooked this house."

Jupiter motioned for silence. There were footsteps in the hall above.

"Farrier forgot to lock the front door," whispered Pete.

"This may get more interesting." Jupiter got up and went to the top of the cellar stairs, where he pressed his ear against the door. He heard, very faintly, a murmur of voices. He held up two fingers, to indicate that two more searchers were among them.

The two men came down the hallway almost as far as the kitchen, then went back again. There were more footsteps on the stairs above. Then a shout, and a sharp crack.

"That was a shot!" said Jupiter.

There was no more shouting, but rumbling voices came muffled to the Dobsons and the Investigators as they waited in the cellar. There were more footsteps on the stairs. Someone stumbled. Then the searchers came into the kitchen and a chair scraped.

"You will sit quietly, and you will not move," said the voice of General Kaluk.

Jupiter backed a step or two away from the cellar door.

The door swung open, and the bulky figure of the Lapathian general filled the doorway.

"So?" said the general. "My young friend Jones.

And Master Andrews. You will come up, please, all of you."

The Three Investigators and the Dobsons came up into the kitchen. The ceiling light was on, and Eloise Dobson gasped at the sight of Farrier, the jaunty fisherman, sitting in one of The Potter's straight chairs, pressing a handkerchief against his right wrist. A splash of red showed on his smart white jacket.

"The sight of blood upsets Madame?" asked General Kaluk. "Do not be alarmed. The man is not badly hurt." He placed a chair for Mrs. Dobson and indicated that she should sit down. "I do not approve of violence unless it is necessary," he told her. "I fired upon this intruder only to prevent his firing upon me."

Mrs. Dobson sat down. "I think we should call the police," she said shakily. "There's a call box on the highway. Tom, why don't you—"

General Kaluk waved her to silence, and the younger Lapathian, Demetrieff, went to stand in the kitchen doorway. He held a gun—an efficient-looking revolver.

"I think, Madame, that we may dismiss this person as being of no importance," said General Kaluk, nodding toward the wretched Farrier. "I was not aware that he was in the area, or I would have taken steps to see that he did not annoy you."

"You sound like old friends," prompted Jupiter. "Or should I say old enemies?"

The general laughed a short, ugly laugh. "Enemies? This creature is not important enough to be

an enemy. He is a criminal—an ordinary criminal.
A thief!" The general placed a chair for himself
and sat down. "You see, Madame, it is my business
to know these things. Among my other duties in
Lapathia, I supervise the national police. There is a
dossier on this person. He calls himself many
names—Smith, Farrier, Taliaferro—it is all the
same. He steals jewels. You will agree, Madame,
that this is a wicked thing to do?"

"Dreadful!" said Eloise Dobson quickly. "But
. . . but there are no jewels in this house. What did
he . . . why are you here?"

"We saw from our terrace, Madame, that this
wicked person seemed to be interfering with you
and my young friends, so naturally we came to
your assistance."

"Oh, thank you!" said Mrs. Dobson. She
bounced up from her chair. "Thank you so much.
Now we can call the police and—"

"All in good time, Madame. You will please sit
down."

Mrs. Dobson sat down.

"I have neglected to introduce myself," said the
general. "I am Klas Kaluk. And you, Madame?"

"I am Eloise Dobson. Mrs. Thomas Dobson.
And this is my son, Tom."

"And you are a friend of Alexis Kerenov?"

Mrs. Dobson shook her head. "Never heard of
him."

"He is called The Potter," said General Kaluk.

"Of course Mrs. Dobson's a friend of Mr. Potter," said Jupiter quickly. "From the Midwest. I told you that."

The general scowled at Jupiter. "Allow Madame to answer for herself, if you please," he ordered. He turned back to Mrs. Dobson. "You are a friend of the man who is known as The Potter?"

Eloise Dobson looked aside. She had the wary look of an unskilled swimmer who suddenly finds herself in deep water. "Yes," she said softly, and her face colored.

General Kaluk smiled. "I think Madame is not telling me the whole truth," he said. "Bear in mind, if you please, that I am an expert at this sort of game. Now, perhaps Madame would care to tell me how she met the person known as Mr. Potter?"

"Well," said Mrs. Dobson, "by . . . by letter. You see, we wrote, and . . ."

"The Potter does a big mail-order business!" said Pete quickly.

"Yeah!" said Bob. "And he mailed stuff to Mrs. Dobson, and she wrote and one thing led to another and—"

"Stop that!" the general shouted to Bob. "What nonsense. Do you expect me to believe that? This woman writes letters to an old man who makes pots, and what they have to write to one another is so interesting that she comes to this small village and moves into his house—and on that day he vanishes? I am not a fool!"

"Don't shout!" cried Eloise Dobson. She was shouting herself. "You have some nerve, barging in here! And I don't care if this Farrier swiped the royal crown of England. We need to get a doctor for him. He's . . . he's bleeding all over the floor!"

The general glanced at Farrier, and at two drops of blood which had dripped on the floor. "Madame is too soft-hearted," he said to Mrs. Dobson. "We will attend to Mr. Farrier when we are ready. Now, you will tell me how you became acquainted with Mr. Potter."

"Well, it's none of your darn business!" cried Mrs. Dobson. "But if you have to know—"

"Mrs. Dobson, I wouldn't," pleaded Jupiter.

"He's my father!" finished Mrs. Dobson triumphantly. "He's my father, and this is his house and you have no business here. And don't you dare—"

The general threw back his head and laughed heartily.

"It isn't funny," snapped Mrs. Dobson.

"Oh, but it is!" chortled the general. He looked up at the younger Lapathian who stood in the doorway. "Demetrieff, we have a real prize. We have the daughter of Alexis Kerenov!"

The general leaned toward Mrs. Dobson. "Now, you will tell me what I wish to learn. Then we will attend to Mr. Farrier, who is such a worry to you."

"What is it that you wish to learn?" asked Mrs. Dobson.

"There is a certain piece of property—a thing of great value—which belongs to my people," said the general. "You know that to which I refer?"

Eloise Dobson shook her head.

"She doesn't know," said Jupiter Jones urgently.

"She doesn't know anything—nothing about Lapathia—nothing at all!"

"Hold your tongue!" snapped the general. "Madame Dobson, I am waiting!"

"I don't know," said Eloise. "Jupiter is right. I don't know anything. I never heard of any Alexis Kerenov. My father is Alexander Potter!"

"And he did not entrust you with the secret?" demanded the general.

"Secret? What secret?" cried Mrs. Dobson.

"Ridiculous!" snorted the general. "He must have told you. It was his duty. And you will tell me—now!"

"But I don't know anything!" cried Mrs. Dobson.

"Demetrieff!" shouted the general, losing his iron control. "She will talk!"

Demetrieff started toward Mrs. Dobson.

"Hey!" yelled Tom. "Don't you touch my mother!"

Demetrieff shoved Tom roughly aside.

"Into the cellar with them!" ordered General Kaluk. "All of them, except this obstinate woman!"

"No you don't!" yelled Pete. He and Bob launched themselves at the younger man, Pete going for Demetrieff's gun and Bob headed in a beautiful tackle at the man's legs.

Demetrieff went down with a loud grunt, and the gun blasted harmlessly toward the ceiling.

That shot was followed by a second thunderous roar. The back door had burst open and The Potter

stood there, an ancient and somewhat rusty shot-gun in his hand.

"Don't move!" shouted The Potter.

Jupiter froze halfway between the cellar door and the chair where General Kaluk sat. The general remained where he was, and Pete and Bob sprawled on the floor on top of the fallen Deme-trieff.

"Grandfather?" said Tom Dobson.

"Good evening, Tom," said The Potter. "Eloise, my dear, I am sorry about all this."

General Kaluk started to get up. The shotgun which The Potter held instantly swung in his direc-tion. "Do not move, Kaluk," said The Potter. "There is a second shell in this gun, and it would give me great pleasure to discharge it right in your face."

The general sat down again.

"Jupiter, my boy!" said The Potter. "Will you please collect the guns? From the general's friend on the floor, of course, and I am sure the general has one someplace. The general has always been fond of guns."

"Yes, sir, Mr. Potter," said Jupiter. "I mean, Mr. Kerenov."

18

The Bargain

No one spoke until Jupiter Jones had taken Demetrieff's revolver, and had searched General Kaluk
and relieved him of Farrier's blunt automatic and
a smaller, but still deadly, pistol.

"Lock the guns in the pantry, Jupiter, and bring
me the key," said The Potter.

Jupiter did so. The Potter tucked the key into a
pocket hidden somewhere in his robe and allowed
himself to relax a bit, leaning against a cupboard.

Only then did Eloise Dobson begin to cry.

"Now, now, my dear," said The Potter. "It is all
over. I have been watching these scoundrels the entire time. I would never have let them touch a hair
of your head."

Mrs. Dobson got up and went to The Potter. He
handed his shotgun to Jupiter and put his arms
around her. "I know, I know," he said. He laughed
and held her away from him, so that she could not
help but see his hair, his beard, and the robe, now
soiled and stained. "Yes, I am a shock to you, eh?"
he said. "No one has a father like Alexander Potter."

Mrs. Dobson nodded, then shook her head, then
burst into new tears.

General Kaluk said something in that strange, singsong language which Jupiter and Bob had heard at Hilltop House.

"I must ask you to speak English," said The Potter to him. "It is so many years since I heard my mother tongue that I am no longer proficient in it."

"Astonishing!" exclaimed the general.

"And who is that?" said The Potter, indicating the unfortunate Mr. Farrier, who still crouched in his chair, holding his injured wrist.

"A person of no importance," said the general. "A common thief."

"His name is Mr. Farrier, Grandfather," said Tom Dobson. "Jupe thinks he's the one who's been trying to scare us out of the house."

"Scare you? How?"

"On three separate occasions," said Jupiter Jones, "flaming footprints have appeared in the house. You will notice three footprints near the pantry and two near the cellar door. There is a third set on the stairs."

"Ho-ha!" said The Potter. "Flaming footprints? I see you've done your homework, Mr. Farrier, and learned about our family ghost. Jupiter, why is the man bleeding?"

"General Kaluk shot him," said Jupe.

"I see. And do I understand correctly that this person has been entering the house and trying to frighten my family?"

"You'll never prove it," growled Farrier.

"He has your extra set of keys," said Jupiter.

"I believe we should summon Chief Reynolds,"

announced The Potter. "My dear Eloise, I had no idea. I was so concerned lest Kaluk might do you some harm, that I neglected to keep a proper watch on my own house."

The general looked at The Potter with some awe. "Do I understand correctly, Alexis, that *you* have been watching *me?*"

"I have been watching you, and you have been watching my daughter."

"May I ask, old friend, where you have been these three days?"

"There is a loft in the garage at Hilltop House," said The Potter simply. "The garage doors are locked, but there is a window on the north side."

"I see," said the general. "I fear I am getting careless in my old age."

"Exceedingly," said The Potter. "And now, Jupiter, let us call Chief Reynolds and have these people removed from my house."

"One moment, Alexis," said the general. "There is the matter of some jewels which were removed from their rightful owners many years ago."

"The rightful owners are the Azimovs," countered The Potter. "It is my duty to safeguard those jewels."

"The rightful owners are the people of Lapathia," said the general. "The Azimovs are gone!"

"You lie!" flared The Potter. "Nicholas did not die in the palace at Madanhoff. We fled together. We were to meet in America. It was arranged. I had a way to send a message to him. I have been waiting."

"Poor Alexis," said the general. "You have waited a lifetime, and for nothing. Nicholas did not even reach the railroad station. He was recognized." The general reached into an inside pocket and produced a photograph. He handed it to The Potter.

The Potter looked at the thing for almost a minute. Then, "Murderer!" he said to the Lapathian general.

The general took back the photograph. "It was not my choice," he told The Potter. "His Highness was my friend, remember?"

"And so you use your friends?" asked The Potter.

"It could not be helped," said the general. "There may be a justice in it. We cannot say. The Azimovs began in blood, they ended in blood. But Alexis, they did end. And what of you? You have spent a lifetime waiting. Waiting behind locked doors. Hiding behind a beard, and the robe of an eccentric. Living without your family. You did not see your daughter grow up, I assume?"

The Potter shook his head.

"For a crown," said the general. "All of this you have done for a crown which no one can wear."

"What do you want?" asked The Potter at last.

"I wish to take it back with me to Madanhoff," said the general. "It will be put into the National Museum there. That is where it belongs. That is where the people wish to see it. It is what the generals promised them so long ago."

"That promise was a mockery!" cried The Potter.

"I know. I know. I myself did not approve, but Lubaski insisted, and once the gesture had been made, we had to go on with it. Anything else would have shaken the faith of the people."

"Liars!" stormed The Potter. "Murderers! How dare you talk about the faith of the people?"

"I am an old man now, Alexis," said the general, "and you are old, too. And the people of Lapathia are happy—I promise you, they are happy. How much love was there for the Azimovs? And now the Azimovs are gone. What will you accomplish if you refuse me? Would you make yourself a thief? I cannot believe it. You have the crown. You swore you would always have it. That is why I came. Give it to me, Alexis, and let us part friends."

"Never friends," said The Potter.

"Then let us at least not part enemies," pleaded the general. "Let us consider what will be the greater good for all. And let us forget the price we have both paid."

The Potter was silent.

"You cannot claim it for yourself," said the general. "Alexis, you have no choice. There is no place it can go but to Madanhoff. And think, what would be the consequences to yourself if it were known that it is in your possession? And what would be the consequences to Lapathia? I do not know, but I can imagine—distrust, unrest, perhaps a revolution. Would you wish another revolution, Alexis?"

The Potter shuddered. "Very well, I will get it for you."

"It is here now?" asked General Kaluk.

"It is here," said The Potter. "Just a moment."

"Mr. Potter?" said Jupiter Jones.

"Yes, Jupiter?"

"Shall I get it?" asked Jupe. "It's in the urn, isn't it?"

"You are a clever boy, Jupiter. It is in the urn. Will you get it?"

Jupe left the room and was gone for perhaps a minute, during which time no one spoke. When Jupiter returned he was carrying a bulky bundle. Layers of soft cloth had been wrapped around an object which Jupiter put down on the table.

"You can open it," said The Potter.

General Kaluk nodded agreement. "I am sure you are curious," he said.

Jupiter undid the wrappings and folded back the cloth. There, exposed on The Potter's kitchen table, was a magnificent crown of gold and lapis lazuli, surmounted by a huge ruby, with a crimson eagle screaming from both sharp enameled beaks.

"The imperial crown of Lapathia!" exclaimed Bob.

"But . . . but I thought that was in the museum at Madanhoff!" said Pete.

The general stood up and looked at the marvelous object almost with reverence. "The one at Madanhoff is a copy," he said. "It is a clever copy, although it was executed without the help of a Kerenov. I suppose there were a few experts, like this . . . this Farrier person . . . who may have guessed at the truth, but the secret has been kept well. The crown is always under glass, of course, and the barriers which protect it are set well back from the case. No one can look too closely at it. Not too long ago a photographer even received permission to include it in his book. He was an expert on photography, not jewels, so we granted his request."

The general began to restore the wrappings to the crown. "The secret will still be kept," he said, "but the crown in Madanhoff will be the real one."

"How can you be so sure your secret will be kept," said the surly Farrier. "You've only got a score or so of witnesses here."

"Who would believe you?" said the general. "You may talk all you wish."

He took the crown and held out his hand to The Potter. The Potter turned away.

"Very well, Alexis," said the general. "We will not meet again. I wish you happiness."

And the general went out, followed by the slim and unsmiling Mr. Demetrieff.

"Jupiter," said The Potter, "I think that now you may summon the police."

19

It Would Make a Keen Movie

A week later Mr. Alfred Hitchcock, the famous motion-picture director, sat in his office and leafed through the notes which Bob had compiled on The Potter and his wonderful secret.

"So the crown was hidden in the urn," said Mr. Hitchcock, "outside The Potter's shop, where hundreds of people came and went every week. That scoundrel Farrier must have passed it a dozen times while he was working so hard to frighten Mrs. Dobson away."

"He told us that he tried to open the urn," said Jupiter Jones. "Of course, he did most of his mischief at night, so he didn't have time or light to examine the urn with care and notice the single-headed eagle looking to the left. The top of the urn came off when you turned it clockwise—to the left. All ordinary containers open the other way. That is the signal which The Potter and the Grand Duke agreed upon when they fled from the palace. If anything happened to The Potter, the Grand Duke Nicholas was to look for a single-headed eagle among a group of the double-headed eagles of Lapathia, and that eagle would be the clue to the whereabouts of the crown."

"And was The Potter planning to take up ceramics even before the revolution in Lapathia?" asked Mr. Hitchcock.

"No," said Bob, who was perched in a chair next to Jupiter Jones. "He became a potter because he had to make a living, but he could have found a number of ways of creating eagles. He could have painted them, or stenciled them on a wall, or . . . or . . ."

"There's always embroidery," put in Pete, who occupied the chair on Jupiter's left side.

"I am sure a scarlet eagle would be most effective in cross-stitch," said Mr. Hitchcock. "Now about this Farrier—your report states that he was arrested by Chief Reynolds on charges of unlawful entry and malicious mischief. I should not think they could hold him long. Will he keep the secret of the crown, do you suppose?"

"He has everything to gain and nothing to lose by keeping his mouth shut," said Jupiter Jones. "Unlawful entry and malicious mischief are minor charges compared to attempted grand larceny. He's in jail in Rocky Beach now, pondering on his sins—which are more numerous than we suspected at first. All those elegant clothes were purchased with a credit card which he found in a wallet that someone had dropped on the street. I am not certain what the charge is for unauthorized use of a credit card, but I should think forgery would enter into it."

"At least," agreed Mr. Hitchcock. "I take it he is strapped for ready cash."

"On his uppers," agreed Bob.

"His car was so shabby," said Jupiter. "It bothered me. It didn't match. He's not even going to be able to pay Miss Hopper for the room he occupied at the Seabreeze Inn. The Potter says he feels responsible, so he's taking care of that bill."

"Most generous," said Mr. Hitchcock.

"Chief Reynolds found the stuff Farrier used to create the flaming footprints in the trunk of Farrier's car, which was parked up the highway out of sight of the house," said Bob. "Whatever it was, he says we'll never know. He thinks it's a good idea not to spread some kinds of information around."

"The man is not without imagination."

"Farrier? No. He has quite a record, and has done time in some of the best prisons. He used to be a crack jewel thief. According to Chief Reynolds, he got too well known. Police everywhere started putting tails on him the second he showed up in any town. Cramped his style. He's been trying to make a living running a little hobby shop in Los Angeles."

"So it was the article in *Westways* which brought him to Rocky Beach?" said Mr. Hitchcock.

"No," said Jupiter Jones. "He told us how he got his first clue to the whereabouts of the crown while we were waiting for Chief Reynolds to come and collect him. He always reads the personal ads in the *Los Angeles Times*. He suspected, as did a number of experts on such things, that the crown on display at Madanhoff was an imitation. He had done some research on the history of Lapathia, and knew about the disappearance of Alexis Kerenov, who was the hereditary guardian of the crown. When he saw the advertisement in the *Times,* with the names Alexis and Nicholas, he remembered the Grand Duke Nicholas who was supposed to have hanged himself during the revolution, and he wondered if it might not have something to do with the crown. He went to the trouble of buying papers from Chicago and New York on a hunch—and he found identical advertisements in them. Then he came to Rocky Beach on a quick visit, and wandered into The Potter's shop one bright afternoon, and . . ."

"And saw the medallion with the eagle," finished Mr. Hitchcock. "That is one thing I do not understand. Why did Kerenov insist on wearing that medallion?"

"He admits it was foolish," said Jupiter. "He felt lonely, perhaps, and it may have reminded him of better times. Also, he felt there was little chance of anyone from Lapathia appearing in Rocky Beach unless they were summoned, and his advertisement—which he placed annually in all the major papers in the United States—was addressed to Nicholas. He felt only Nicholas would understand it. It was part of the agreement which they made when they fled together from the palace at Madanhoff. They would separate and both try to make their way to the United States. Alexis would advertise once a year, on the anniversary of the revolution, until Nicholas found him. And if anything happened to Alexis before Nicholas found him, Nicholas could always examine the files of back editions of various newspapers and would, at least, know in which town Alexis had settled. Then he was to look for the odd eagle with the single head."

"An involved scheme," said Mr. Hitchcock, "and one that left a great deal to chance. However, I suppose they did not have a great deal of time to work out anything more practical with a revolution going on around them. So for a lifetime Alexis waited."

"And Nicholas never escaped."

"What was the photograph which the Lapathian general showed The Potter?" asked Mr. Hitchcock.

"He wouldn't tell us," said Pete. "Something gruesome."

"And proving that Nicholas was dead, no doubt," added Jupiter.

"It must have been a great shock to The Potter," said Mr. Hitchcock. "On the other hand, he must have begun to suspect that his vigil was in vain. So many years had passed."

"I guess he hoped right to the end that Nicholas would show up, and the Azimovs would be restored to their throne," said Bob.

"In which case," chuckled Pete, "The Potter would be the Duke of Malenbad, and Mrs. Thomas Dobson of Belleview, Illinois, would eventually get to be a duchess. I wonder how Mrs. Dobson would enjoy being a duchess."

"Has she forgiven her father?" asked Mr. Hitchcock.

"Yes," said Bob. "She's still there, and she's helping him in the shop. She and young Tom will stay until the end of summer."

"And the Lapathians have departed?"

"They left the minute they got their hands on the crown," Jupiter reported. "We have to rely on guesswork with the men from Lapathia. We can only assume that the *Westways* article led them to The Potter. I think that they rented Hilltop House planning to wage some sort of war of nerves on The Potter. It upset them greatly when he disappeared and a young woman and a boy moved into his house. But they kept watching and waiting until they saw Farrier make his move, out there in The Potter's yard, and then they came scrambling down that hill to make sure nobody got the crown before they did.

"General Kaluk, I am sure, was sent to Rocky Beach because he had once known Alexis Kerenov, and might be better able to recognize him than Demetrieff, who never knew him personally. And he did recognize him, in spite of all the beard and the white hair. The Potter had not changed that much, and Kaluk had changed scarcely at all."

"It would make a keen movie, don't you think, Mr. Hitchcock?" asked Pete. "I mean, flaming footprints and a family ghost and an innocent daughter who doesn't know what the score is, and stolen jewels!"

"It has some points to recommend it," said Mr.

Hitchcock. "There are still one or two things you have not explained in your report, however. The sound of water running in the pipes in The Potter's house when all the taps were off."

"That was The Potter using the outside faucet," said Jupiter. "He could not hide out in that old garage without water, and since the Lapathians never left Hilltop House, he couldn't get water there. He had to come to his own house at night. He did not want to reveal himself to Mrs. Dobson, however, because he felt that the less she knew, the better off she would be. The Lapathians could not see him at the faucet, even in the moonlight, because of the thick hedge of oleanders behind the house. It was for that reason that they could not see Farrier, who entered and left by the back door."

"How did Farrier get into the house to get the keys?" asked Mr. Hitchcock.

"That was ironical," said Jupiter Jones. "The Potter was apparently so preoccupied with preparations for the Dobsons that for once he neglected to lock up tight. Mr. Farrier claimed he had no trouble getting in the front door—only had to pick one lock. He told Chief Reynolds he was just curious about the house, and that later, when Mrs. Dobson snubbed him, he grew angry and tried to frighten her with the flaming footprints."

"And the police chief of Rocky Beach believed him?" said Mr. Hitchcock, with some astonishment.

"Not at all, but no one has come up with a better story, so he has to take what he can get."

"One other detail," said Mr. Hitchcock. "You were fired upon when you came down from Hilltop House. Was that Farrier?"

"No," said Bob. "The Potter again. He apologized. He wanted to scare us off, since he felt the men at Hilltop House were dangerous. He had had that shotgun stored in the shack where he kept supplies, so he had no trouble getting his hands on it when he wanted it."

"What do you think?" insisted Pete. "Wouldn't it make a great movie?"

Mr. Hitchcock sniffed. "No love interest."

"Oh!" Pete subsided.

"However," said Mr. Hitchcock, "Alexis Kerenov, the Duke of Malenbad, has been reunited with his daughter, so at least we do have a happy ending."

"She's a great cook," said Jupiter. "The Potter's putting on weight. And he went into Los Angeles and bought a suit of clothes and some shoes. He's going back to Belleview with Mrs. Dobson in the fall to meet his son-in-law, and he doesn't want his daughter's friends to think he's . . ."

"A nut," put in Pete.

"Eccentric," said Jupe. He paused. "Which he certainly is."

ALFRED HITCHCOCK
and The Three Investigators Series

Available in paperback

The Secret of Terror Castle
The Mystery of the Stuttering Parrot
The Mystery of the Whispering Mummy
The Secret of Skeleton Island
The Mystery of the Fiery Eye
The Mystery of the Silver Spider
The Mystery of the Screaming Clock
The Mystery of the Moaning Cave
The Mystery of the Talking Skull
The Mystery of the Laughing Shadow
The Mystery of the Flaming Footprints
The Mystery of the Shrinking House

Available in hardcover

The Mystery of the Green Ghost
The Mystery of the Vanishing Treasure
The Secret of the Crooked Cat
The Mystery of the Coughing Dragon
The Mystery of the Nervous Lion
The Mystery of the Singing Serpent
The Secret of Phantom Lake
The Mystery of Monster Mountain
The Secret of the Haunted Mirror
The Mystery of the Dead Man's Riddle
The Mystery of the Invisible Dog
The Mystery of Death Trap Mine
The Mystery of the Dancing Devil
The Mystery of the Headless Horse

All titles also available in Gibraltar Library Binding.
All editions published by Random House, Inc.